BIG DATA IS WATCHING YOU!

Also by Bruce Hartman:

Perfectly Healthy Man Drops Dead

The Rules of Dreaming

The Muse of Violence

The Philosophical Detective

A Butterfly in Philadelphia

Potlatch

The Devil's Chaplain

BIG DATA IS WATCHING YOU!

Bruce Hartman

"My goal is not to predict the future, but to prevent it." – Ray Bradbury

Swallow Tail Press

Big Data Is Watching You!

First Revised Edition, 2018
Alternative title: *I Am Not A Robot*

Published by Swallow Tail Press
Philadelphia, PA, USA
www.swallowtailpress.com
Also available in ebook format

Front cover photo courtesy of Shutterstock.com

ISBN-10: 0988918153

ISBN-13: 978-0-9889181-5-3

PUBLISHER'S PREFACE TO
FIRST REVISED EDITION (2018)

In the three years since this book was first published, Silicon Valley has advanced its agenda of world domination to the point where many of the author's observations no longer seem fanciful or amusing. In keeping with Moore's Law, we expect that new editions will be necessary every two years, then every year, then every month, day, week and finally every minute and second until the Satirical Singularity — the moment when satire *becomes* reality — will have occurred. Anticipating that event, we have moved the book to our Non-Fiction list. We expect that it will be ruthlessly suppressed. Not only will it be deleted from the internet: it will become permanently irretrievable and invisible to all search engines — in other words, *it will never have existed.* Thus we offer this first revised edition with the urgent recommendation that it be purchased immediately, read quickly, and committed to memory if any doubt remains in the reader's mind that the conditions described in the book are coming to pass. Although the word "comic" has been omitted from the subtitle, we hope that until the Satirical Singularity occurs (and this will be a measure of how close that moment is) the attentive reader will find something to smile at in the book.

❂

Chronicler's Note: The Legal Department has requested that we make the following disclosures: Chicken® (patent pending) and egg® are registered trademarks of Monsanto Company. Gravity™ and The Solar System™ are trademarks of The Walt Disney Company. All other words and phrases in this book are Copyright © by Google Inc., owner of the Alphabet™ and English® (except in Canada™).

PART I

1.

Smith stared back in confusion when Julia said he was living in a dystopia.

"A dystopia?" he repeated. The word was new to him. "What do you mean?"

They were somewhere in the Green Mountains, walking on a dirt road through a strangely silent woods. That was all Smith knew. He'd lost his way in the hills, his car stopping short where a huge fallen tree blocked the road. The woman who introduced herself as Julia climbed over the fallen tree before he could tell his car to turn around. Surprisingly, she offered to walk him into the nearby village to find something to eat. The eerie silence followed them into the village, swallowing his thoughts. Julia looked different from anyone he'd ever seen, though she had (he soon realized) the same blond hair and blue eyes and the same awkward gait as everyone else in the village. The others—he noticed half a dozen villagers cutting weeds or stacking firewood around a row of decaying frame houses—weren't nearly so friendly as she was. Most of them turned away or receded into the shadows rather than look at him. Some of them, he realized with a start, had beards.

"It's a society where, basically, life sucks," she explained. "You have no freedom or privacy. You can't do anything, you can't say anything, you can't even think without somebody spying on you or listening in."

Smith didn't want to seem condescending, but he couldn't help feeling superior to the lowlifes he'd noticed slinking away as Julia led him into the village. These were apparently her neighbors. Who was she to cast aspersions on his life in Google Earth?

"My life doesn't suck," he said, smiling as always. "In fact, I can't imagine being happier than I am. I have a good job at Celebrity Solutions, a nice condo, hundreds of friends on Fakebook, and two wonderful pets. Everything I want is delivered to my door within thirty minutes by an Amazon drone."

Julia rolled her eyes. "Guess who drank the Kool Aid!"

"Kool Aid?" Kool Aid® was Smith's favorite beverage.

"Try thinking an original thought and see what happens."

He stared back uncomprehendingly.

"You know," she teased. "Say something more than 140 characters long."

What was she talking about? Did she seriously expect him to violate the Terms of Service? She spoke fluent English® but used words he'd never heard before, like "freedom" and "privacy." He'd heard that connectivity could be poor in rural areas, where the inhabitants—known as "Yahoos"—often expressed eccentric, paranoid ideas. Obviously, for whatever reason, he and Julia weren't connecting. Still, there was something about her that affected him in a surprising, unfamiliar way. He later learned that it was called "sex®."

Julia wore unusual clothes, the kind of clothes (Smith assumed) typically worn by Yahoos: tight blue trousers on the bottom and a tight red shirt on the top, in each case disclosing unsightly bulges in places where women were ordinarily indistinguishable from men. Everyone knew that there was no difference between women and men, apart from the applicability of certain pronouns. For this reason he attributed the peculiarities of Julia's physique not to her sex but to poor connectivity.

Absorbed in such thoughts, he followed her to the ramshackle wooden structure she called home, which, oddly, she shared with two other people. "My parents," she called them. "They're out baling hay with Uncle Floyd. I can't do that because I'm allergic. What do you want to eat?"

"Have you got any Froot Loops®? Or Captain Crunch®?"

"Cold cereal? We haven't had any deliveries up here for about three hundred years. I don't think I'd like it anyway."

Smith blushed in embarrassment. "You can't not *like* something!"

"Sure I can." Her expression curled downward, concealing all her teeth. "There's lots of things I don't like."

His breath tightened, as it did sometimes at the office when he could feel his co-workers' disapproval swarming around him. Nothing buzzed in his mind, though, and he felt isolated in the silence, even though Julia stood beside him. "But you can't *say* you don't like something!"

"OK, whatever." To his relief, her face had brightened back into a normal shape. "I like you, anyway. I'll say that."

He felt shaky, unsteady on his feet. "Look, I've got to be going."

She reached out and touched his hand. "Will you be back next weekend?"

On the way home in his car, Smith tried to make sense of Julia. He liked her, of course, but meeting her in this strange village had left him feeling uneasy. She talked as if she didn't know anyone was listening. True, the grid was patchy up here (which explained the eerie silence) and it was a long way for Customer Service to travel in the event of a problem. But he couldn't help wondering if it went deeper than that. Julia's odd physique, coloration and facial expressions he could attribute to diet or genetic variation, but what about those people with *beards?* What could be the explanation for that? He'd seen a few old science fiction movies, and he remembered a few—*Jersey Shore* came to mind—that took place in prehistoric times and featured troops of *hominids,* those evolutionary ancestors of the human race who could walk and talk and even reason to some extent but whose lifestyle had been unimaginably revolting. Everyone assumed that they'd gone extinct, but when he saw those people with beards (should he even call them *people?*), he'd had the sinking feeling that he might have stumbled into a village of hominid survivors. But what about Julia? Did that mean she was a hominid? When she reached out and touched his hand, he knew he wanted to see her again.

As his car sped toward home, Smith replenished his faith with a silent prayer. Big Data, as always, was watching him.

2.

As the Chronicler of Google Earth, I take all of history as my domain. I could start my story in hominid times, or with the birth of Barney Google or the Great Stench, but having been inspired to begin in the middle of things, I'll set my cursor here: at Smith's chance encounter with Julia on that long-ago summer afternoon. Things would have turned out much differently if Smith's car had sped him back to his condo in Nusquama, his job at Celebrity Solutions, his beloved guppies Mot and Derf, before Julia climbed over that fallen tree. And Julia, had she not been dissatisfied with her life in Coolidgeville, might have hidden in the foliage and watched Smith speed away without even offering him a snack. What happened instead—this seemingly insignificant meeting of a man and a woman—marked a turning point in human affairs.

Did you see any of this coming, Smith? Could you have imagined the temptations and ordeals that lay ahead of you? Of course as the Chronicler I know how the story ends. But I'll try to put myself in your place and view the world as it must have appeared to you then.

Everything in your world—from your coffee maker to your toothbrush to your thyroid to your hypothalamus—was connected, but the connections were hidden from you. If you noticed them they appeared as oddities of nature, like rainbows or caterpillars turning into butterflies, guided by the invisible hand of Big Data. You thought you understood Google Earth, but your understanding of it was almost completely false, as you would soon discover. In fact you were living your life in a fog—or more accurately, a cloud.

We'll resume our chronicle on the morning after your accidental visit to the Green Mountains. Your encounter with Julia had entered history, innocently, with no suggestion of its consequences. Having noted it, I'll step back and let you get on with your life.

3.

Long before Smith woke up, his condo had been the scene of feverish activity on the part of his furniture and appliances. The kitchen cupboard, having noted a shortage of desiccated carbohydrate flakes, and the refrigerator, which had discerned a dwindling supply of simulated fat-free bovine extraction, had joined forces to notify Amazon, which promptly dispatched a drone containing the needed supplies. His mattress had recorded his sleep patterns, body weight, pulse and blood pressure, and relayed this information to the Cloud. At sunrise the blinds flew open and lights flashed over his bed, propelling him to the kitchen table, where fresh coffee cooled in his mug and a bowl of Rice Krispies® crackled instructions to the toaster. After breakfast he showered and dressed for work, which took a little longer than usual. His cereal spoon, having detected bad breath, had dispatched a signal to his toothbrush, recommending that it spend more time on the lower left molars. The green tights and tunic that he wore every day (and which identified him as a Level 5 Publicist) had detected body odor, dandruff and toenail fungus. Fortunately all these conditions could be remedied by Big Data before he reached the office.

Owing to these delays, Smith found himself still at home when the cleaning crew arrived. An intensifying buzz caught his attention as a squadron of insect-size drones descended on the building and surged into his condo through special ports in the walls and the floor. As he watched with satisfaction, an army of robotic ants marched over the kitchen counters, harvesting stray crumbs, while a swarm of flies cleaned the carpet. Snails slurped their way around the bathtub and cleaned the toilet. Miniaturized hermit crabs popped out of holes in the floor and set about making his bed. A mechanical raccoon knocked over the garbage can, pulled out the plastic liner and dragged it outside.

It was a typical day in the best of all possible worlds.

At the office, people didn't really need to talk. Everyone knew what everyone else was thinking, whether they talked or not. Sometimes Smith's supervisor, O'Brien, hovered over him and he felt uncomfortable with her disapproval buzzing around him—he wished she would just say what was on her mind (even though he already knew what it was) so he could get back to work. O'Brien was a woman and his secretary, Bosworth, was a man, so for O'Brien he said "she" and "her" and for Bosworth he said "he" and "his." He liked O'Brien, of course, but she could be annoying before a big sacrifice if she thought he didn't have the messaging under control. Bosworth had been his secretary for about a hundred years and Smith had yet to figure out what he did, other than playing video games; he earned only 500 data units a month, yet somehow managed to download some pretty glamorous vacation photos to his Fakebook page. Here at Celebrity Solutions—where Smith worked as a Level 5 Publicist—everyone was expected to pull their weight. There were sacrifices to arrange, Celebrities to cage and feed while they waited for the big day, lions and other wild beasts to keep under control. On a day like this, the day of a major sacrifice, he took justifiable pride in his work, even if O'Brien thought he was a moron. He was doing his part to make Google Earth a better place.

When he told people he worked at Celebrity Solutions, they always asked if he felt sorry for the Celebrities when they were thrown to the lions. In truth he felt more sympathy for his two pet guppies, Mot and Derf, than he did for those pathetic losers. They whined about their hardships—about not having lives of their own, about being pursued by paparazzi and hounded by fans—but let's face it, if they weren't Celebrities, they would have been nobodies. They were famous for being famous, selected and trained for the roles they were meant to play in the sacrifices. They learned to put on special clothes and masks and wigs so they could imitate the all-time greats—Pelvis Wrestly, Urethra Spanklin, Lady GooGoo—who hadn't been seen for hundreds of years, if they ever existed. And after Smith had written his press releases, posted his videos on YootTube, tweeted "#ThumbsUp OrDown?" for Bob Dillweed or #ThrowHer ToTheLions?" for Linsey Lowhand or Scarlatina Johnnson— after the public had made its choice and the lions had done their work, these people, who started out as Beast Folk earning 500 data units a month at McDonalds, ascended directly to the Cloud to sit at the right hand of Big Data, along with Barney Google himself. And you were supposed to feel *sorry* for them?

Smith didn't actually think any of those mean thoughts, of course. They were just in the air, buzzing around the office like flies. Everybody was thinking them (except the part about Mot and Derf, which was his contribution), so nobody could be blamed for not liking the Celebrities. You couldn't not like them. You couldn't not like anyone.

He glanced up at the posters on the wall—PRIVACY IS SHARING and FREEDOM IS CONNECTIVITY—and felt unimaginably grateful to be back in the office, away from the maddening silence of the Green Mountains. Another poster—CHOICE IS OBEDIENCE—reminded him that this was where he belonged. And then there was the big sign arching over the doorway: BIG DATA IS WATCHING YOU. When Smith was feeling a little anxious, as he was this morning after his weekend adventures, that was the thought that gave him the deepest comfort. Whatever happened, Big Data was there, in the Cloud, watching over him.

O'Brien breezed up beside him and the bad vibes started right away. She'd noticed some unusual thoughts in his feed, recollections of his encounter with Julia and her village in the Green Mountains. He smiled and said hello, but before he began to share his thoughts, her eyes told him she knew all about his weekend, or thought she did—he quickly realized that she knew only what had happened before his car stopped at the fallen tree: she knew nothing about Julia, nothing about the village. Julia had talked as if no one was listening, and apparently she'd been right. The whole valley must be off the grid, Smith realized, which was supposed to be impossible in Google Earth. But don't let O'Brien catch you thinking about it, he told himself—they say she's got a back channel to Higgs. No, think about something else, concentrate on the sacrifice that's scheduled to start in a couple of hours: Okra Windfree, Taylor Snifft, Mira Nightly—the usual publicity hounds. That's your job, that's what you're supposed to be thinking about. O'Brien squinted at him attentively, trying to make sure he was thinking about the sacrifice.

"All thought feeds may be monitored and recorded for quality control purposes," she reminded him before she glided away.

4.

Some have wondered how Smith—so two-dimensional, so boring and dim-witted, as he seemed at that time—could have made such an impact on the world. When he met Julia he was hardly a well-rounded individual, or even an individual at all, but rather a mere cell in the social network whose only saving grace, from Julia's point of view, was a kindly twinkle in his eyes suggesting (contrary to what she'd been taught about Flatlanders) that he was not a soulless automaton. Julia had a rich inner life that no one in Coolidgeville suspected. At the age of twenty-three, still unmarried, she was melancholy but secretly hopeful that she could find a way to live without sacrificing the dreams and tender emotions she'd hidden deep in her heart. She'd discovered the names for those emotions—and the fact that other people shared them long ago—in the ancient books her ancestor Smoky McLuggage had sealed up in the old church building. No one in Coolidgeville seemed to know that such feelings existed, not even her parents, well-meaning as they were. She was the only one who realized that a whole world of human sensibility had been extinguished when Coolidgeville went off the grid. Her parents were suspicious, dull-witted and prejudiced. They wanted her to marry her cousin Griff, whose main claim to fame (though it was shared by his brothers Garth and Grant) was that he could fit his entire fist inside his mouth, a performance invariably followed, as soon as he removed it, by a peal of maniacal laughter. Griff and Garth and Grant and all the other men in the valley were given to outbursts of violence, bullying, jealousy and greed. They didn't like being called Yahoos, but that (as Julia knew from her reading) was exactly what they were.

Julia had liked Smith from the first minute she saw him. With that kindly twinkle in his eyes, he seemed so innocent and good-hearted, if not obviously very bright. He was tall, athletic and handsome, which put him miles ahead of Griff and all the other men in the valley, who were uniformly short, fish-eyed and gnome-like in appearance. Besides, they were all her cousins, all McLuggages and Breedloves and Thigpens and Proudfoots, with the worst traits of each clan exaggerated by generations of inbreeding. Smith was a Greek god compared to any of them, even if he was a Flatlander. Her Uncle Floyd had warned her about Flatlanders. "They're robots," he told her, "under the control of WiFi waves, with the attention span of a Rhode Island red. Not one of them can say a sentence that's more than 140 letters long, including spaces." That might be true of Smith—in fact, based on their first meeting, she had to acknowledge that Uncle Floyd could be right. But it wasn't an insurmountable defect, especially as compared to Griff, who communicated mostly in grunts, growls and grimaces. She had thousands of old books Smith could read to increase his attention span and expand his vocabulary, if she could just keep him away from those WiFi waves. The bigger problem was that Smith, like all Flatlanders, seemed totally uninterested in sex. He was like a ten-year-old in his naiveté and underdevelopment. But she knew how to address that problem, if he would just come up to see her again the next weekend.

One night after work Smith wandered in the deserted mall where the retail stores used to be, a vast hulking ruin overgrown with vines and weeds and scrubby trees. A Google van patrolled the perimeter with its rooftop camera rotating—luckily, this one didn't have a gun turret—and a Federal Express drone buzzed overhead. There were a few disreputable stores that remained open for business. One of them, Charrington's Antiques, sold a lot of junk that nobody wanted and did a brisk trade renting out contraband movies, including some of the older ones about hominids. Try as he might to push the thought from his mind, he was still troubled by the suspicion that Julia and her village might be hominid survivors.

He slipped into the shop casually, as if he happened to be walking by and something in the window caught his eye. The shopkeeper, Charrington, slouched behind the counter watching some recent sacrifices on his screen, occasionally muttering encouragement to the lions. He paid no attention as Smith walked in and started inspecting a quaint Apple iPad, as if considering an acquisition for his antiques collection. On the wall hung an old poster, showing a bald grinning man in a double-breasted suit. The poster's message—"I Like Ike"—was redundant: whoever Ike was, you couldn't not like him. Smith sidled up to the counter and cleared his throat in hopes of attracting Charrington's attention. The shopkeeper kept his eyes fixed on the screen. "Help you find something?" he grunted.

"I was wondering," Smith said in a low voice, "if you might have any movies for rent?"

"Something the matter with your screen?   Can't get streaming?"

"No, not at all. I just wondered if you had any"—Smith moved his lips without making any sound—"science fiction. You know, like time travel to prehistoric times."

"Hominids?"

"That's right. Hominids."

Charrington leaned so close that Smith could see little beads of saliva shooting out of his mouth. "Hominid movies are all trash," he said, "but some are a lot worse than others. Some of them show hominids *eating!*" He groped under the counter and pulled out a small flash drive, which he slipped into a brown plastic bag. "I won't say *what* they're eating—I don't use that kind of filthy language."

Smith pulled out his wallet and reached inside. "How much?"

"I might let you borrow one of these movies," Charrington grumbled, "but I wouldn't be renting it to you. I'd be letting you borrow it, friendly-like, in exchange for a small donation"—he handed the plastic bag to Smith—"a hundred data units, for example, for three days. But I won't describe it to you, especially the food those creatures ate. Certain words will never cross my lips!"

"I understand," Smith agreed, slipping him a 100-unit card. He stashed the little bag in his pocket and turned to leave. "I almost forgot," he said, spinning back around. "What's the name of the movie?"

In the tiny interval that elapsed after Smith turned away, Charrington's face had contorted into an ugly sneer, which vanished as quickly as Smith spun back toward him.   "The name of the movie?" he smiled. *"It's a Wonderful Life."*

Smith watched *It's a Wonderful Life* that night after all his neighbors had gone to bed and the din of the thought feed had subsided. He felt a little ashamed of himself, though he couldn't imagine what harm could come of watching a movie. Still, he was glad the movie was so out of date and the hominids so unbelievable. He was especially relieved—after Charrington's tirade about food and filthy language—that there were no references to "F-----f----s" or "p----a," and the characters weren't shown eating anything that was obviously non-GMO. The town in the movie, Bedford Falls, looked like a bigger version of Coolidgeville, where he'd met Julia. The women wore funny clothes and seemed to have some of the same bulges as Julia. Other than that, the movie didn't shed any light on whether Julia was a hominid. She definitely seemed a lot smarter than the hominids in the movie.

He played a few of the most exciting scenes again and then watched some of his favorite shows on TV. They came on automatically—*Teenage Mutant Ninja Turtles, The Muppets, Frankenweenie*—but on impulse he switched to a different channel and watched *Sponge Bob,* a show he'd never seen before. Watching *Sponge Bob* was an innocent, seemingly harmless mistake, but it was one he would soon regret.

5.

Two nights later Smith sat in his condo—it was actually a single room: a screen and three cinder block walls, with one tiny window over his bed—working on his Fakebook page. When he signed in, as usual, he faced a screen that showed him the statement "I am not a robot" and asked him to prove it by clicking on little boxes that contained pictures of cars or street signs. He'd always done that, without thinking much about it, but that night for some reason he asked himself, 'What would I do if I *were* a robot?' and the answer seemed clear: he would click on the little boxes to prove that he *wasn't* a robot, because that's what he had to do to sign in. So does that mean I *am* a robot? he wondered. If I wasn't a robot, I wouldn't always say 'I am not a robot.' Sometimes I might say 'I *am* a robot'... no, that's ridiculous. It can't be that the only way to prove you aren't a robot is to say that you are! This was all very confusing. And so—without thinking any more about it—he just skipped the question, and to his surprise he was allowed to continue on to Fakebook. It was a decision he would later regret.

Smith's life, like everyone else's, was defined by what appeared on his Fakebook page, and living it consisted of adding new posts to his timeline. He lived the most successful, glamorous life he could afford on the salary of a Level 5 Publicist. Photos of a vacation at the Outer Banks (currently located in Tennessee) could cost up to 2,000 data units; pictures of ski vacations in Costa Rica or New Guinea cost over 3,000 units; and, at the upper end (well beyond Smith's range), a one-minute video of himself cavorting on a beach in Kansas with a bunch of Senior Management types would run well into six figures. Job upgrades, unusual talents, gourmet meals in fancy restaurants—posting these on your Fakebook page required enormous numbers of data units. Friends, too, did not come cheaply. You could be friends with your co-workers for a small investment in data units (unfortunately this came with the obligation to view cute pictures of their pets and to like everything they did); college friends cost a little more (obliging you to like and comment on their fictitious career achievements); but being friends with glamorous people you had never met, such as Senior Management figures like Higgs, could cost thousands. If you wanted it all—an exciting career, exotic vacations, powerful friends—you had to purchase the Premium Package, which ran upwards of 10,000 data units a month. Luckily—and this was what made it all worthwhile—no one on Fakebook was allowed to not like you or anything you claimed you did.

Just after Smith had finished posting a photo of Zimbabwe and a heartfelt description (downloaded from YootTube) of his fictional experiences there helping the Zimbabweans preserve the habitat of the spotted elk beetle, he heard a knock on the door. Opening it, he found two people (a man and a woman, as he later concluded, based on pronouns) wearing long dark raincoats that were held together by a complicated system of belts, buckles and flaps. The man was tall, smiling and friendly, but the woman was short and squat and mean-looking, with big hair like some of the hominids in *Jersey Shore*.

They used the polite formal greeting—"Big Data is watching you!"—and Smith replied in kind. The man held up a leather folder displaying an official badge. "Customer Service," he smiled. "Mind if we ask you a few questions?"

Suddenly Smith's worst nightmare—everyone's worst nightmare—was coming true: a knock on the door and a couple of Customer Service Representatives barging their way into his condo. "Where were you on the night of June 14, at approximately 11:00 p.m.?" the friendly one asked.

"I... I was at home," he stammered. "Watching TV."

The woman with the big hair smirked knowingly at her partner. "What show did you watch?" she asked Smith. "Do you remember?"

"Sure. It was *Sponge Bob.*"

"*Sponge Bob,* eh? And how'd you happen to pick that show?"

"I don't know. I just I thought I might like it."

"They say that every time. Well, did you like it?"

"I... I don't know," Smith stammered, suddenly understanding the danger he was in. On the one hand, you couldn't not *like* something—Customer Service would never put up with that—but on the other hand, the woman seemed intent on tricking him into admitting that he'd violated the Terms of Service.

"No, of course you don't know," she said. "You were out of profile, weren't you?"

Again he hesitated, hoping the friendlier representative would come to his rescue. "I just felt like watching it, that's all."

"You knew you were out of profile, didn't you?"

Fortunately the friendlier representative chose this moment to intervene. "Customer Smith," he said in a gentle voice. "Don't you think we know what you like by now? You like *Teenage Mutant Ninja Turtles,* so we know you'll like *The Muppets.* You like *The Muppets,* so we know you'll like *Frankenweenie.* We know you, Customer Smith. We know you better than you know yourself. And trust me, based on your viewing profile there's no reason to believe that you'd like *Sponge Bob.* "

Smith felt stubborn and unwilling to concede, even though he knew it was hopeless arguing with a Customer Service Representative. "I thought it was worth a try," he said.

"But it couldn't have been, could it, Customer Smith? Your profile is who you are. You can't just start being somebody else because you get the notion."

The woman lunged forward and grabbed Smith by his shirt-tail (she was too short to reach his lapel). "You know what can happen to customers who go off profile?" she snarled. "You could get put on hold. Do you realize what that means? On hold!"

"No, please!" Smith begged. "That—"

"We've got operators standing by in Bangalore, Baghdad, Bala Cynwyd—"

"No, please, I—"

"You want to change your profile, why don't you give them a call? They'll put you on hold before you can spit out your UPC code. Is that what you want to happen?"

"No, absolutely not."

"All right, then. Try to stay on profile in the future."

Before they disappeared through the door, the man turned and beamed at Smith one last time. "Is there any other way we can be of service to you today, Customer Smith?"

After the Customer Service Representatives had left, Smith sat trembling in front of his screen. That week at the office he'd seen Smedley transferred to Omaha, Jones given a package, Blair suddenly departing to spend more time with his family—and since nobody knew what a family was, what could that mean but termination of service? He felt ashamed of himself for not sticking up for *Sponge Bob*—actually he had enjoyed it quite a bit—but he knew he'd be asking for trouble if he admitted to liking a show that was off profile. And to think, all this just because he'd watched *Sponge Bob!*

Thank Big Data they didn't ask about *It's a Wonderful Life.*

6.

Julia waited for Smith by the old fallen tree, cradling the .22 caliber rifle she used for squirrel hunting. It was a beautiful June morning, the kind that makes a girl's heart throb with love, if she knows anybody worth throbbing about. Griff, who wanted to marry her, only made her want to stay in bed and hide under the covers. That was her melancholy streak, her mother said, as if it was something that would end, like a lucky streak when you're playing cards. But it never ended, it only got worse, especially when she thought about the miserable choices her life seemed to offer. At that moment, though, standing in the shade under a big sugar maple, listening to the birds twittering and the crickets chirping and the bees humming in the wild flowers, and hoping an unsuspecting squirrel might cross her path so she could shoot it, all she could think about was how beautiful life can be if you just let it take you where it's going. She'd found a whole collection of poetry books in the old church building she inherited. Most of the poems didn't make much sense, but she'd read a few that struck a chord—she hesitated to say it—in her soul. That was another thing people never mentioned that she'd learned about in those old books: your soul. She didn't know what it was, but she was sure she had one.

At exactly noon Smith's car cruised up the dirt road and slowed to a stop. He climbed out and hopped over the fallen tree, without noticing her under the sugar maple. She didn't move or say anything, but waited to see what he would do next. He was just as tall and handsome and cheerful as she remembered—about 28, she guessed, though he had the mentality of a ten-year-old. Her Dad had warned her about that. Flatlanders are like overgrown kids on their way to summer camp. Maybe it's hormones that make you age, she thought, because Smith sure didn't have many of them (unlike Griff, who smelled like a rutting moose and could hardly keep his hands off her if he thought nobody was looking). Well, if lack of hormones was the problem, she had a pretty good idea what to do about it.

Smith seemed excited to see her, though he didn't try to hug or kiss her or even hold her hand. They chatted for a few minutes and she led him toward the village. At a crossroads they turned up a steep hill, passing a corn field on one side and some curious black and white cows on the other. Before long they came upon a congeries of trailers, tarpaper sheds, rotting woodpiles and rusted oil tanks, in the middle of which slouched a rundown cabin with a wide front porch. Three bearded men sat on the porch strumming banjos and ukuleles. In front of them stood a man in blue denim overalls whose appearance was so freakish that Smith could only stop and stare. He had wrinkled, blotchy skin, a bald head and a grin full of missing teeth. In fact he was merely old, a condition Smith had never before had occasion to observe.

"Howdy, Julia!" the old man shouted, stepping out to greet his visitors.

The three younger men, all of them pale and a little fishlike in appearance, nodded at Smith with undisguised hostility.

"This is my uncle," Julia said. "Floyd Thigpen."

"Flatlander, eh?" Uncle Floyd said.

"A Flatlander is the word they use around here for somebody that comes from down below," Julia told Smith. "Nothing personal."

"Nothing personal," Uncle Floyd agreed. "See that microwave tower up there?" He pointed to the top of a distant hill, where an antenna peeked above the trees. "Built by my great-grandfather to the nth degree—who was also named Floyd Thigpen—about four hundred years ago. Old Floyd didn't have much truck with the government or the media or big companies generally, but he had a tractor and a backhoe and a crane for well-drilling and taking down trees, so the phone company hired him and his three sons, Garth, Griff and Grant"—he gestured toward the three bearded musicians perched on the porch—"these here are my sons, named Garth, Griff and Grant just like his—and they built that tower for the phone company, which is what they had back then, phones, instead of all those wireless gadgets the Flatlanders started using after that. Now old Floyd, as I say, he didn't much like the phone company or Flatlander companies in general, and he had a hunch as to what they were fixing to use that tower for, so when he and his sons built it they rigged up a little tin pie plate—if you climb up there you can still see it today—that blocks out the valley from being bombarded by microwaves. In those days they used those waves to control phones, and then it was computers, next it was cars, and before long they were operating people by remote control, right from that tower. Turned people into robots, is what they did."

A quick glance at Julia told Smith that Uncle Floyd was dead serious. "So," he hesitated, "they're sending out waves and operating you as if—"

"Not us," Uncle Floyd glared. "You. We're off the grid."

"I'm not sure I understand this," Smith said. "How could waves from that tower be controlling people?"

"Why, with all the little sensors and receivers and transmitters they've planted in them! In you, I mean. You don't think you have them? You're a Flatlander, ain't you?"

Nothing personal, Smith reminded himself. Yahoos were known for their eccentric personalities and xenophobic world-views. Garth, Grant and Griff sat nodding behind their beards, perfectly in tune with Uncle Floyd's paranoid vision of the world.

"If you don't believe me," Uncle Floyd said, "ask Julia. She knows all about this, don't you, Julia?"

To Smith's discomfort, Julia nodded as if she agreed with him completely.

"You ever use a computer?" Uncle Floyd asked Smith. "Take a look at Google Earth or street view or whatever they call it now. Coolidgeville just looks like a flat, empty space. Nothing there. It doesn't exist as far as they're concerned."

Smith felt compelled to speak up. "They?" he asked. "Who are you talking about?"

"The government. The media. Google. You've heard of Google, haven't you?"

Asking Smith if he'd heard of Google was like asking if he'd heard of Gravity™ or The Solar System™. He'd heard

of English®, too, and Fakebook® and Twitter® and the
other basic institutions of society (all of which were Google
subsidiaries), but so what? Did that mean they were part of
some wacky conspiracy to turn people into robots? What
were these shadowy entities Uncle Floyd kept talking about—
the "phone company," the "government," the "media"? Did
they exist outside the old man's fevered imagination? Smith
was a Level 5 Publicist with an income of over 100,000 data
units a year, and he was confident that if such things existed
he would know about them. And there was something even
more troubling about Uncle Floyd, something sinister and
frightening which Smith had been trying not to notice: he
sounded like some Yahoo follower of Goldstein, the
subversive arch-enemy of everything that made life in Google
Earth worth living. How could Julia associate with a
terrorist?

"Warn't always like that, you know," Uncle Floyd rattled
on. "Warn't always some government or phone company
telling people what to do. Folks were just folks, deciding for
themselves, one minute after another, what they were going
to do next."

"That's still how it is, even for us Flatlanders."

"People were as free as birds. Like those sparrows you
see swooping around over there, twittering at each other
without a care in the world. They don't need some
government telling them where to swoop."

Smith knew better than to argue any further. He wished
Uncle Floyd a pleasant day, nodded to Garth, Griff and
Grant, and followed Julia back down the hill. "Uncle Floyd's
got it about half right," he told her. "Those sparrows can

swoop around like that only because of Big Data. It's the same for people."

"For Flatlanders, maybe," she said. "Up here we don't have those waves controlling us."

He stopped and turned to face her. "Don't you understand, Julia?" He didn't want to sound condescending or preachy, but he had to save her from Uncle Floyd's dangerous delusions. "It's Big Data that links everybody together and makes sure everything's the way it's supposed to be. Big Data even looks out for those sparrows. They may seem to fly around at random, but not a single one falls to the ground without Big Data knowing about it in advance."

Smiling, she took his hand and led him farther down the hill. "Come on. I want to show you something."

At the bottom of the hill they took the main road toward the village center, where an old white building with a kind of tower on top stood in the middle of a neatly mown lawn. "It used to be a church," Julia said, "a long time ago. Then it was a bookshop."

"A what?"

"Where they sold books," she laughed. "You've heard of books, haven't you?"

Smith had never heard of books, and more amazingly to Julia, he had never heard anyone laugh. (In Google Earth, laughter was a privilege of Senior Management, exercised only behind closed doors.) "Why did you make that braying sound?" he asked her.

"Laughing? You laugh when something is funny. When something seems absurd."

He still didn't understand—in Google Earth, nothing seemed any more absurd than anything else—but he hoped the mystery would be dispelled if she showed him a book. "Can we go inside?"

Julia led him into a dusty, cavernous space lighted by colored glass windows. The walls were lined with shelves bulging with small objects of various colors, most of them about an inch thick and eight or ten inches high. "These are books," she told him. "Uncle Floyd says this is all that's left of western civilization. My ancestor Smoky McLuggage inherited the building from an uncle of his who'd collected about twenty thousand books and stored them in here. Smoky turned it into a second-hand bookshop. That was before there were computers or Kindles or anything like that."

Julia reached toward a shelf and took down a book written by a woman named Thomas Jefferson. (Smith knew Thomas Jefferson was a woman because of the long wavy hair that covered her ears.) "Remember when I first met you," Julia said, "I asked if you could say something more than 140 characters long?"

"That would violate the Terms of Service," he winced. "I'm only authorized to use English® up to 140 data units per message."

"But you could say something that's more than 140 units if you wanted to, right?"

"Sure. But why would I want to?"

She thumbed through the book until she found the page she was looking for. Then she handed it back to Smith. "Here. Try this."

He held the book open and read aloud: *"We hold these truths to be self-evident, that all men are created equal, that they are endowed by their Creator with certain unalienable Rights, that among these are ..."*

His voice faltered as he reached the 140-character limit. *"Life..."* He rubbed his eyes and stammered: *"Lib-Lib-Lib-Lib..."*

"It's OK. You don't need to finish."

He forced himself to cough out the next few words: *"Lib-Lib-Liberty and the pur-pur-suit of Hap-Hap-Hap..."*

"Happiness," she finished for him. "Life, Liberty and the pursuit of Happiness."

Sweat poured off his forehead, his heart pounded, his knees weakened. "What does that mean?" he yelled. "It doesn't make any sense!"

He stumbled to a wooden chair and sat down. "That book has words in it I've never heard before. Like some of the ones you use—what did you say when I first met you? *Dystopia?* I looked that up. It's not in Google Dictionary. And I'll bet those aren't either: *Rights. Liberty. Happiness.*"

"Those words are in a lot of these books," she said.

"But they're not allowed! Haven't you familiarized yourself with the Terms of Service? If they're not in Google Dictionary, no one is allowed to use them."

"Not even Senior Management?"

"I doubt it very much. And look at this: the *Creator.* What are they talking about? Big Data?"

"No, the Creator is something else."

"What else could it be? Big Data watches over us, takes care of us, makes sure everything's right. Who else could the Creator be?"

Julia lowered her eyes. "There's no such thing as Big Data," she said gently.

"What are you talking about?"

"It's just a giant computer somewhere."

"A computer? What are you talking about?"

"I've read a lot of these books that were left over from western civilization," Julia said. "There isn't a word in any of them about Big Data."

"You call that a civilization?"

"They're full of sentences longer than 140 units, though."

"No wonder their civilization collapsed! Nobody could finish a thought."

Julia took Smith on a walk through the woods to her favorite pond, where they sat together on a log holding hands and talking about their philosophies of life. When they'd exhausted that topic—which in Smith's case took about fifteen seconds—she showed him how to shoot the rifle. He had never seen a gun before, or even known that such things existed. Julia set up an old tin can on a stump and knocked it off with her first shot. She handed Smith the gun and stood close behind him, wrapping her arms around him as she taught him how to peer through the sights and aim the rifle. He fired a shot, which made him jump back into her arms and cover his ears. She laughed and kept hugging him until he pulled away. When they were done shooting, he followed her back out of the woods and down a shady dirt road to her house. Dogs, cats and chickens roamed the yard, but apart from them the village seemed to be deserted. "Everybody's at a potluck supper down at the Grange Hall," she said. "We have the house all to ourselves."

Taking his hand, she led him up a rickety flight of stairs to her bedroom, which was decorated with Celebrity posters: Johnny Depth, Marlon Drano, George Gooney. He was tempted to boast—being anxious to make a good impression—that he'd played a role in the sacrifice of some of those very Celebrities. But before he could open his mouth, she peeled off her shirt (she wore nothing under it) and stretched out on the bed, reaching her arms toward him.

"Are you going to bed already?" he asked. "It's only six o'clock."

"Come on," she beckoned.

"But I'm not sleepy."

She grabbed his hand and pulled him down beside her, and then rolled over and pinned him down with a long, passionate kiss. He wondered what she was doing. Is this how she kept her lips moist? Did she think he needed mouth-to-mouth resuscitation? Was there something on his teeth? Then it dawned on him that she was *kissing* him. This was something he'd seen in some old hominid movies.

She ran her fingertips lightly over his face and down his chest and around his neck—he assumed she was checking him for ticks—and then she kissed him again, even harder, before pulling away. "Don't you even know about sex?" she asked.

"Sex®?" It was a registered trademark of the Walt Disney Company—that was about all he knew. "Wasn't that something hominids used to do?" he asked warily.

"Birds do it," Julia smiled. "Bees do it. Even educated fleas do it."

Smith had no sense of humor. He rolled away from Julia and sat up. "I need to ask you something," he said. "I don't know how to say this, because I like you, Julia, but—you're not a hominid, are you? You and the others here?"

"We're people. People just like you, only—"

"Only what?"

"You're different."

I'm different? he thought. That's a good one!

Evidently Julia decided not to go to sleep after all. She pulled her shirt back on and led Smith downstairs to the kitchen. "What you need," she told Smith, "is some good old-fashioned, red-blooded home cooking. I'll fix you a dinner you'll never forget."

He sat at the Formica-topped kitchen table watching in fascination as she sliced potatoes into thin strips on the countertop, heated up the oven and poured some oil into an iron skillet. The food sizzled and cracked and had a delicious tangy smell that was new to him. "I'll tell you something I'd never tell anyone else," he said. "I've seen some of those hominid movies. I rent them at an antique shop called Charrington's."

Julia stood at the stove with her back turned. "OK," she said, glancing over her shoulder. "Do me a favor? Go there this week and ask for *Horny Asian Housewives* or *Debby Does Dubai*. Will you do that for me?"

"I don't know," he hesitated. "I got a visit from Customer Service just for watching *Sponge Bob*."

She turned to face him. "What are you afraid of?"

"Are there going to be dirty words in those movies?"

"There might be," she admitted.

"There are certain words," he stammered, "that without even knowing what they mean, you just instinctively know never to say. They're bad words, dirty words. I'm afraid Customer Service will be listening."

"Why would they be listening?"

"Everything is monitored and recorded for quality control purposes."

When a bell chimed, Julia opened the oven and pulled out a round crust covered with cheese, tomato sauce, and salty disks she called pepperoni. She sliced it into wedge-shaped pieces and slid several of them onto his plate. The smell was heavenly—it made him want to seize the pieces with his teeth and gobble them without using his knife and fork, which is something he'd never been tempted to do with the desiccated carbohydrate pellets he got from McDonalds.

"Be careful, that's very hot!" Julia warned him. "Blow on it first."

He savored another delightful whiff. "What is this?"

"I call it Italian cheese and tomato pie."

"I wish I owned the patent on it!"

She turned away with a sly smile.

"It *is* patented, isn't it?" he asked, a little alarmed. "I mean, this stuff didn't just come out of the ground or something, did it?"

"No, of course not. Don't be ridiculous!"

The pie tasted even better than it smelled. The first few bites filled him with a heady sense of physical power that he'd never experienced before. "What else are we having?"

Julia pointed to the skillet on top of the stove. "Salisbury steak on a bun, with ketchup. And"—she lifted a basket of potato slices from a vat of sizzling oil—"every man's favorite: Liberty strips."

Liberty—there was that word again. What did it mean? Something to do with potatoes, no doubt. Smith pounded the table with the handles of his knife and fork and chanted: "Liberty strips! Liberty strips!"

"The way to a man's heart is through his stomach," Julia said.

"What does that mean?" Smith asked.

"You'll find out!"

7.

As Caesar and Emperor Omnipotent (CEO) of the East, Higgs was the most powerful human in Google Earth. He lived fifty stories above street level at the East's most fashionable address, Google Towers, in exclusive downtown Nusquama. His 16-room, three-story penthouse had a private elevator and a rooftop garden, a gym, tennis courts, an outdoor hot tub and three balconies looking over the Sea of Shells toward the buried remains of Bean Town. On a clear day he could see the upper stories of the old John Hancock Tower, looming like a flat, rectangular island in an ocean of gigantic clam and oyster shells. People who lived in Nusquama before the Great Stench—the few who survived it—claimed that in those days Bean Town was a center of science and technology. This Higgs found hard to believe. Hadn't it been a team of so-called experts from the Medieval Institute of Technology (MIT) who came up with the mollusk idea in the first place?

Not that he had anything against science. *Au contraire* (it was part of his brand to pepper his speech with words and phrases from dead languages), he had reached his position at Google not through sycophancy or cut-throat office politics (although he excelled at both) but through his brilliance as a scientist. Science was the only reason there were any people left alive. Some claimed that science, through its pathologically blind disregard for the consequences of its advances, had brought about most of the disasters it now boasted of mitigating. That, in Higgs's view, was an ungrateful and short-sighted view of human progress.Pathologically blind it may be—*psycho*pathologically blind, some might have said—but science was just another name for rationality. If science was psychopathic, then he was proud to call himself a psychopath, one of those rare individuals who aren't hindered by irrational fears or sympathies and can therefore cultivate a rational mind. He did not consider himself evil, or mean, or in any way anti-social. (At Google, being evil would have violated the company motto.) *Au contraire,* he felt that his objective outlook, together with his superior intellect, qualified him for the leadership position he had achieved. He prided himself on always doing the right thing, which means doing whatever is necessary to bring the greatest good to the greatest number. Few leaders have the presence of mind to put that truism into practice. Throughout history, the most evil people, judged by their impact on the world, have been those with the loftiest aspirations. For that reason Higgs knew that he had to tread carefully. He had to make sure he wasn't getting sentimental or utopian or vain, lest he delude himself with the idea that he was heroic or saintly or even the savior of mankind (though admittedly—and it must have contained more than a grain of truth or he wouldn't have needed to be on guard against it—that idea had crossed his mind).

Recently he'd been brooding on a bold, innovative solution to all the world's problems. One summer evening as he sat on his balcony contemplating the Sea of Shells, listening to iTunes (his favorite kind of music was algorithm and blues), the Next Big Thing had suddenly hit him. Come to him—him alone—right out of the blue! There it was, staring the whole world in the face, and he was the only one who knew what to do with it. That, he reminded himself, is why they paid him the big data units. Why he sat on top of Google Earth, second only to Big Data itself!

For now, his big new idea would have to be Hush Hush, Top Secret, For His Own Eyes Only. He couldn't talk about it with anyone, except of course his closest confidant, Ralph. Giving credit where credit was due, he acknowledged that Ralph had played a decisive role in nurturing this innovation. Life at the top had been lonely until Higgs discovered Microsoft YesMan™, developed by one of Google's subsidiaries exclusively for CEOs. He downloaded it to his 18-karat gold Apple EyeWatch® and a friendly, supportive voice—which he named "Ralph"—was with him twenty-four hours a day, seven days a week. Rain or shine, his YesMan™ was there to help him wrestle with his toughest decisions. When asked a question, Ralph always answered "Yes" or words to that effect, never presuming to disagree—he was just a machine, for Big Data's sake!—unlike some of the junior executives Higgs had been obliged, unfortunately, to transfer to Omaha.

Like everyone in Senior Management, Higgs was exempt from the most annoying features of modern life while still enjoying all its benefits. His thoughts and messages weren't recorded (even for quality control purposes) or limited to any set number of data units. He had perfect health, a great physique and high self-esteem, freedom from disease, aging and negative emotions, all without the sacrifice of a sex life. The penthouse was protected by a domelike tin roof that blocked reception of the WiFi signals everyone in Google Earth received from Big Data suppressing their natural sex hormones and desires. Constantly exposed to those signals, the populace—male and female—had no interest in sex or even knew that it existed. But a few minutes under the tin roof usually had a liberating and overpowering effect on the women Higgs brought there from the Junior Anti-Sex League. Once the hormones and desires were released from years of suppression, they often ran riot, as if the women—and Higgs supposed this would apply to men too—were making up for lost time.

His current mistress was a cute mid-level manager at Celebrity Solutions named O'Brien who'd caught his eye at a meeting of the Junior Anti-Sex League. (The women in the Junior Anti-Sex League, in their plaid kilts and knee socks, had always been especially attractive to Higgs.) The last time O'Brien had taken the elevator up to his penthouse—it was their fourth *rendezvo*us under the tin roof—he noticed that she'd affected a certain proprietorial air, as if she thought she belonged there. She even suggested that in due course Higgs might transfer her out of Celebrity Solutions so she could live full time in the penthouse. That wouldn't be possible, of course, but this particular morning wouldn't be the best time to break the news. He had received some information from Customer Service about one of O'Brien's reports at Celebrity Solutions.

Higgs could tell O'Brien was in a bad mood as soon as she stepped off the elevator in her plaid kilt and knee socks. He wrapped his arms around her and tried to force a kiss.

"Not this morning," she said, turning away. "I don't feel like it. I've got a headache."

"A headache?" he chuckled. "How quaint!"

She faked a smile, making sure he knew it was fake, and sat down on one of the six couches in the living room where they had sometimes made love. In case she'd left any doubt about the mood she was in, she held her arms crossed as if gearing up for battle.

"What's the matter?" Higgs asked.

"I like being with you. You make me feel like a real woman. But I don't like this switching back and forth. I come here, we have sex, and then it's back to la-la land. Why can't I stay here all the time? Or do you just want me for the sex? I'm a person, you know."

He smiled his warmest, most loving, most accepting smile, the one he'd perfected for situations just like this one. But inwardly he was disappointed and not a little annoyed with O'Brien. Whatever she had to say, he'd heard it all before, from countless other women: You just want me for sex; I'm a person, you know. Yes, she was a person and she was quickly outliving her usefulness. It happened to all of them sooner or later, usually sooner. You get them under the tin roof, show them what they've been missing, and before you know it they're acting like Lady GooGoo. Did this woman realize she could be transferred to Omaha with a flick of the fingertip?

Higgs had been waiting for the hormones to take effect, and already she was showing signs of warming up. The next arrow in his quiver was business talk, which was sure to turn a woman on.

"I'm sorry," she said. "I feel that something's missing in our relationship. Shouldn't people who are doing what we're doing have *feelings* for each other?"

Higgs sat down beside her and squeezed her hand. "All that emotional nonsense was eliminated long ago," he said. "People used to have a lot of stupid *feelings* that caused nothing but conflict and customer dissatisfaction. A lot of those feelings were tied up with sex."

"Is that why sex was eliminated?"

"Absolutely. It's all in the corporate history."

He leaned over to kiss her as he unbuttoned her blouse. "If you go back a few hundred years, society was dominated by *consumers*—that's what customers were called then. Consumers welcomed every new technology that promised to improve their lives. When some new gadget or innovation came on the market, they bought it—why do you think Google controls everything?"

O'Brien turned toward him, kissing him hungrily. She reached her hand inside his shirt and mimicked what he was doing to her. "Phone apps, nano-cameras, sensors, implants, social networks," he said, laying on the business talk. "People flocked to them as if they had magical powers. And look what they could do! Regulate metabolism, fine-tune brain chemistry, perform gene therapy, reverse aging, cure cancer, eliminate unhappiness and other negative emotions—they could do all that and more. The apps kept getting smaller and smaller, until at last there were nanobots and nano-sensors embedded in every part of the human body, exchanging signals with remote servers according to algorithms controlled by Big Data, so you weren't even aware of the miracles they were performing inside you."

"Inside me?" she giggled as his hand went lower. "But what about sex? People didn't sign up to have that eliminated, did they?"

"Not exactly, but after all those other improvements had made them practically immortal, they couldn't very well keep on reproducing, could they?"

She wriggled out of her jeans and pulled him down on top of her.

"First reproduction," he said, stroking her leg, "then sex itself had to go. The process was so gradual that for a long time people hardly noticed, or at least they didn't talk about it. They were so happy and healthy: no illnesses, no death, no aches or pains, no negative emotions—why worry about a little loss of libido? And of course it wasn't only physical. Attitudes had to change as well."

"I know all about that," she said breathlessly. "I'm Outreach Chair of the Junior Anti-Sex League, remember?"

"I almost forgot about that!"

"I still don't see why you had to stamp out sex," she gasped, nibbling his earlobe.

"The sex hormones—and the whole sex relationship— threw everything out of kilter. You wouldn't believe how complicated the endocrine system turned out to be. And how connected everything was to sex. Those *feelings* you were talking about—they were too erratic, too unpredictable, they interfered with all the algorithms. The whole thing had to go. For both men and women."

"But how? How did you do that?"

The situation was heating up beyond the capacity of words to describe it, but not beyond Higgs's capacity to spin them out. "The breakthrough came when Monsanto patented the first GMO food product that turned off the sex hormones," he explained, breathing heavily. "I think it was some kind of Greek yogurt. After that, progress came quickly."

"Not too quickly, I hope," she gurgled.

"Traditional non-GMO food—especially what they called 'fast food'—had the potential to destroy everything we'd achieved. The stuff acted like an aphrodisiac, blocking the incoming anti-sex signals from the servers. It had to be kept away from teenagers (that's what they called the Beast Folk in those days) at all costs! If they never tasted it, they'd remain innocent of sex forever. So those non-GMO fast foods had to be banned—and not only banned, but suppressed, stigmatized, anathematized!"

"But for Senior Management...?"

"There was an exception, obviously. We all live under tin roofs and eat whatever we want." He took a deep breath as he headed into the home stretch. "But for society in general, even the *words* for those non-GMO foods had to be stamped out. Those words—they're really the only dirty words left in the language, aren't they?"

"Yes!"

As they writhed together in ecstasy, he whipped himself into a frenzy by flashing the worst of those words on a mental PowerPoint slide: *P---a, h--------s, f----- f----*. "I can't even bring myself to say them to you while we're having sex!"

"Come on!" she panted. "Say them! Say those words to me!"

"You mean it?"

"Yes! Yes!"

"Pizza!" he murmured in her ear. *"Hamburgers! French fries!"*

"Ohhhhhh!" she moaned. "Yes! Ohhhhh... Yes!"

After they had finished, the lovers lounged in Higgs's outdoor hot tub sipping cool drinks as they watched the morning sun blaze over the Sea of Shells. Higgs realized that in the heat of passion he might have been a little carried away with his business talk. Some CEOs grunt like animals during sex, others conjure images of fantasy lovers. Higgs liked to talk about business. It was what he cared about most, the only thing, in fact, that really stirred his soul. In his enthusiasm, he realized, he'd revealed far too much to O'Brien about the past—information that only Senior Management had access to. It wasn't the first time this had happened—there was a whole subdivision near Omaha inhabited by his former mistresses living under new identities—but when it came to telling an attractive woman about Google's history, he just couldn't help himself. And so when O'Brien, glistening naked in the hot tub, started asking the kinds of questions no one was supposed to ask, he opened up and poured his heart out to her.

"What happened to money?" she asked. "Didn't there used to be something called money?"

"It went away," he told her. "Just like that." He snapped his fingers to emphasize the suddenness and finality of this event. *"Voilà!"*

"But how?"

"It happened on a Wednesday morning at ten o'clock. All the money in the world, which had been converted into BitCoin by order of the Bank of China, suddenly disappeared. Banks and stock exchanges halted operations and everyone was sent home from work. The authorities assumed that the money had been transferred to secret accounts in the Cayman Islands and would soon be recovered. But they had no inkling of the seriousness of the disaster. The money had simply been deleted, as a practical joke, by a teenage hacker in Papua New Guinea. The hard-drive of the world economy had been wiped clean."

O'Brien relaxed for a few minutes in the surging bath as she absorbed this information. She let her eyes range over the Sea of Shells to the east, the impenetrable forest to the north and the rolling countryside to the south, dotted with condominium complexes and deserted malls. In all directions, about five miles apart, stood the towers.

"Have the towers always been here?" she asked casually.

Higgs shot her an unpleasant glance. Even for him, pillow talk had its limits. "Yes," he said. "The towers have always been here."

"But weren't they built by Google? Or one of its affiliates? I mean, they look man-made."

"Google has always been here," he said. "Google is not man-made."

"What about the Sea of Shells? Has it always been here?"

"No," he laughed. "That was a Monsanto project. It was before Monsanto was a Google subsidiary," he added.

"How did that happen?"

Higgs knew he shouldn't answer, but as usual he couldn't resist the urge to talk business to an attractive woman, especially a naked one beside him in a hot tub. "At one time," he told her, "people believed that global warming due to higher levels of carbon dioxide in the atmosphere would bring about an environmental catastrophe."

"Is that what happened? Is that what the Sea of Shells is?"

"Ironically," Higgs said, sweat dripping off his forehead, "when the catastrophe came, it was caused by an attempt to stop global warming."

"I don't get it."

"As you may know, mollusks—such as clams, oysters and snails—absorb carbon dioxide from the atmosphere to form their shells. Dr. Byron T. Jorgenson, a brilliant invertebrate geneticist at MIT, working under a grant from Monsanto, saw in this phenomenon the solution to global warming. By altering the gene that controls the growth of mollusk shells, Dr. Jorgenson and his team were able to speed and enhance the growth of these carbon-fixing shells a thousand fold. Unfortunately, the gene found its way into the ocean before it could be fully tested. The mollusks it engendered were so large and fast-growing that in a few months the oceans were filled with them. Clams and oysters twenty feet in diameter were a common site along the coasts, spitting sea water fifty feet into the air. And the presence of all those mollusks heated up the sea water, so instead of cooling, the climate heated up; currents and wind patterns shifted, deserts consumed farmland and forests."

"Didn't anyone do anything to stop it?"

"There was a strong public backlash, of course," Higgs explained. "Clam chowder was banned in New England, *conchiglie* in Italy, *escargots* in France. But it was too late: the changes could not be reversed. The government—there was a government in those days—announced that the earth would soon be uninhabitable, except for oysters, clams, and mussels. Monsanto, trying to minimize its losses, filed a patent on *bouillabaisse.*

"And then, in a reversal worthy of a Greek tragedy, the giant mollusks, like the humans who had engineered them, outdid themselves. The oceans, clogged and polluted by their shells and effluents, became so hot that they evaporated. Without water, all the mollusks (and all other forms of marine life) died. There was great rejoicing, but it lasted only a few days, until the Great Stench began. As the mollusks rotted in their shells, humans retched and choked to death by the millions. It was the greatest mass extinction since the dinosaurs."

Higgs grabbed a towel and wiped the sweat from his forehead. "And worse was yet to come: the water that evaporated from the oceans blocked the sun, condensed over the poles and fell as snow, forming glaciers to begin a new Ice Age. Sea levels dropped all over the world as vast quantities of water were locked into ice."

Until that morning O'Brien had never wondered about the origins of the Sea of Shells or the glaciers that covered Canada, Europe and Asia. She'd assumed that they were always there, like Walt Disney World and Google Earth itself. Now she sipped her drink in numbed recognition of the truth about the past, her questions silenced by the enormity of the horrors Higgs described. Idle curiosity had led to a devastating loss of innocence.

Higgs tried to cheer her up. "Now that I've told you all this, I'm going to have to kill you," he laughed. "Or upgrade you to Senior Management."

O'Brien reminded herself not to take any of this too seriously. It was in the past, if it had even really happened. Higgs was just weird enough that he might be making it all up, just for the thrill of telling her about it. If he thought he owed her an upgrade for listening, so much the better—that was her only reason for staying with him. Now that her visits to the penthouse had awakened the sleeping giant inside her, she knew he wasn't the only man in the world, and certainly not the most attractive. There were plenty of others she'd rather sleep with: tall, athletic-looking men she saw on the street or in her condo complex, even Smith at the office...

Her reverie ended when Higgs broke in to say that no upgrade would be forthcoming in the near future. For the time being he wanted her to continue working at Celebrity Solutions. "Do you have a guy named Smith reporting to you?" he asked. "I need you to keep a close eye on him."

"Smith? He's a moron!"

"Of course he's a moron. But he's been flagged as a troublemaker."

8.

O'Brien returned to the office in a pensive mood. At best she felt indifferent toward Higgs: if she'd been reviewing him on Amazon, he would have been lucky to get two stars. But (as he liked to remind her) he was the most powerful man in Google Earth. He was her ticket out of this dead-end job. Though biologically in her late twenties for the past 300 years, she'd lost her virginity just a few weeks before, on her first date with Higgs. He invited her to his penthouse, ostensibly to honor her contributions to the Junior Anti-Sex League. But no sooner had she stepped off the elevator than he proceeded to a hands-on demonstration of everything she'd spent her life militating against (of which, it turned out, she'd had but a vague and anatomically incorrect understanding). What happened next certainly came as a surprise! The Junior Anti-Sex League, she learned, had been founded by Higgs in order to lure girls in plaid kilts and knee socks up to his penthouse. Apparently everyone (outside of Senior Management) was bombarded day and night with WiFi signals that suppressed any interest in sex. Higgs's tin roof worked by blocking those signals, triggering physiological changes that could never be reversed. And now that she'd had this experience (albeit with Higgs, who, even in her novice estimation, left much to be desired in most performance categories), how could she go on living in this sterile, childish world?

For some reason Higgs wanted her to keep a close eye on Smith. Evidently Customer Service had observed him going off profile, watching TV shows that hadn't been recommended. But was that something the CEO of the East should be worrying about? "There must be more to it than that," she told Higgs, hoping he'd reveal more about his secret new project, which he called the Next Big Thing. Higgs answered evasively: "Smith is a useful idiot"—O'Brien agreed with that, except for the "useful" part—"Keep an eye on him. He's a good looking man, isn't he?" Yes, he was unusually handsome, tall and muscular. But so what? Weren't all the men outside of Senior Management just a bunch of pre-pubescent little boys? Smith seemed different from the others, though. Last week she'd noticed some static in his thought feed, as if he didn't want to share his mental processes. And this morning, back from another weekend in the country, he seemed to be acting strangely. For one thing, he couldn't keep his eyes off her breasts. Maybe there was hope for him yet.

Smith had been experiencing unusual symptoms ever since he left Julia's the night before. The dinner she served him— Italian cheese and tomato pie, Salisbury steak on a bun with ketchup, liberty strips—had been unexpectedly delicious, but it left his stomach feeling nervous and fluttery, and that morning, after a night of tossing and turning in his bed (something he'd never experienced before), his whole body felt restless and jittery, as if each part had a mind of its own. Even after a hearty breakfast of Froot Loops and Captain Crunch, he felt a lingering hunger, an unfamiliar craving not for more cereal but for something he couldn't identify. His mouth felt dry and his teeth ached as he arrived at the office. The first thing he noticed was O'Brien, or more specifically certain parts of O'Brien that he'd never noticed before.

When Julia, in her bedroom the night before, had pulled off her shirt and sprawled on the bed, he'd noticed her breasts, of course. But he'd paid scant attention, concerned as he was with whether she might be a hominid. That was before she'd served him that delicious dinner, which he now realized, with a sinking feeling, must have been contaminated with unpatented, non-GMO ingredients. How else could it have made him so sick? He felt weak and light-headed, as if his stomach might sink and his mind fly out of control. Before him stood O'Brien, with whom he'd worked every day for as long as he could remember. Suddenly she looked different. Remembering Julia in her bedroom, he realized that O'Brien, who was also a woman, must look the same under her clothes as Julia. In fact he could make out the curves of her breasts and hips as she patrolled between the cubicles, monitoring the thought feeds of her reports. He followed her with his eyes, abruptly lowering them when she turned toward him. She glared at him as if she knew what he was thinking, which of course she did. For the first time in his life he felt ashamed.

Higgs paced in his rooftop garden, conferring with his wristwatch. Ralph was unusually argumentative that morning, reflecting the latest updates to Microsoft YesMan™.

Higgs made a note to discuss this with the President of Microsoft. Yes, diversity was Google policy, but did he really need his assistant telling him "That kicks ass!" or "Fo' shizzle my nizzle!" when a simple "Yes" would have been sufficient?

"I have a meeting later today with the Board of Directors," Higgs said. "Naturally I'd like you to attend."

"I'll be there," Ralph agreed.

"It's about my new idea. I'm hoping I can get the Board to go along with it. Could be a bit of a hard sell."

"I doubt it," Ralph said.

"What you do mean, you doubt it? Aren't you supposed to agree with me?"

"I am agreeing."

"You are not!"

"I'm disagreeing that it will be a hard sell, which means I think it's a good idea."

"You think it's a good idea?"

"Absolutely."

"All right, then." Higgs disliked backtalk from Ralph, but the discussion was too important to cut short. "Let me bounce it off you and see what you think. The human race has been around for about 200,000 years, a relatively short time as species go. Even the Neanderthals lasted longer than that. Now in those millennia since modern humans appeared, there's been endless war, slavery, exploitation, economic folly, destruction of the environment. Enough to demonstrate, if any doubt existed, that humans are a brutal, irrational, stupid and generally nasty species."

"Couldn't have said it better myself," Ralph agreed cheerfully.

"Right." That was a little more agreement than Higgs wanted to hear from a machine, but he went on: "So what do we do about it? Science and technology have accelerated at a blistering pace. We know more today about any single individual than was known in the year 2000 about everyone who had ever lived."

"Altogether the most pernicious race of little odious vermin that nature ever—"

"That's enough!"

"I'm agreeing with you," Ralph objected.

"No, you're not, because you're not listening. My point is this: To a very great extent, people have been transformed into data points and algorithms. When they cease to exist as physical organisms, they live on in the Cloud as part of Big Data. Couldn't that process be accelerated? Isn't that the answer to their wars, their depravity, their environmental destruction? To be taken up in the Cloud—like sacrificed Celebrities—into a purified,   more ethereal level of existence?" Higgs gestured in the direction of what had been Bean Town, where the top floors of the John Hancock Tower seemed to float on the Sea of Shells. "A lesser man," he went on, "a less innovative spirit, gazing from his balcony over that vast graveyard of oysters, scallops and clams, would have seen nothing but a *bouillabaisse* of extinct, genetically modified mollusks. But what I saw was the Next Big Thing. I saw the Next Big Thing and I wanted Google to be leading the way."

"This is brilliant, Higgs!" Ralph said. "You've outdone yourself!"

"The Next Big Thing is extinction!" Higgs crowed, the glint of madness in his eyes. "The extinction of the human race!"

Ralph emitted a low, pulsing laugh. "When do we start?"

9.

As the week wore on, Smith found himself tormented by anxiety and shame. He felt the lingering effects of his dinner with Julia—insomnia, a nervous stomach, a blind craving he couldn't understand—and the embarrassment of being caught, several times an hour, staring at O'Brien's breasts. Do all women have breasts? he wondered, or was O'Brien a hominid too? Maybe that was why she gave him that sly smile, as if the two of them shared a secret no one else could know. In the morning, when he took his shower, he looked down at his own body and felt ashamed. What was doing this to him? Was it something in the liberty strips?

Fortunately Bosworth, his secretary, didn't notice anything going on between him and O'Brien. Bosworth sat at his work station absorbed in video games, his favorite being *Demonic Drone Destroyer,* which involved launching missile attacks based on incoming data from Federal Express drones. Bosworth boasted that he'd scored more kills than any other player in Google Earth.

"Who are you killing?" Smith asked, without knowing exactly what *killing* meant.

"Just a bunch of Yahoos!" Bosworth growled. As a lifelike rural landscape rolled across his screen, he launched an attack on a pickup truck carrying crates of non-GMO chickens. The truck exploded and chicken feathers filled the air, eliciting a delighted howl from Bosworth.

Smith might have joined in the fun, but he had serious work to do. Another big sacrifice was set for later in the week, and his publicity work had fallen behind schedule. He'd been having flashbacks from the book by Thomas Jefferson that Julia made him recite from. When he tried to write about the Celebrities, the words that kept popping into his mind were "Life, Liberty and the pursuit of Happiness," which didn't sound consistent with being thrown to the lions. True, being sacrificed was the whole point of the Celebrities' existence, and he'd never wasted any time fretting about them, any more than Bosworth fretted about the make-believe Yahoos he blew up in his video games. But for some reason—oddly connected in Smith's mind with the shame he felt about staring at O'Brien's breasts—he'd started worrying about the Celebrities and wondering if they deserved to be sacrificed. He tried to shield these thoughts from O'Brien and even from Bosworth and his other co-workers. Hoping to put his mind at rest, he decided to visit the pens beneath the Stadium where the Celebrities were kept.

The Stadium was constructed, like everything else in Google Earth, from fragments of mollusk shells salvaged after the Great Stench. It had a hundred entrances, five hundred seating sections, a thousand Greek yogurt stands and a hundred thousand clam-shell seats. It could hold the entire population of Nusquama and have space left over for the Celebrities and the wild beasts that were essential for the sacrifices. And everyone knew that if the sacrifices were not performed precisely as tradition required, Big Data would disappear from the Cloud and all life in Google Earth would perish.

At the Celebrity Solutions portal, Smith used his badge to gain admittance to the Substadium and the catacomb-like tunnels where the Celebrities were caged. As always he was amazed at how many cages there were and how many Celebrities were held in each one, grouped together as they would be when they were sacrificed. Those whose sacrifice dates were nearest on the calendar were already in costume— clothing, wigs, masks, even make-up—and required to stay in character, perfecting the movements, voices and mannerisms of the famous figures they'd been chosen to represent. In the first cage Smith stopped at, he saw a number of familiar faces: Pelvis Wrestly, Lady GooGoo, Beyondée, Kam Kardashiam, and Bob Dillweed, who stood tuning a guitar. They met Smith's stare with expressions of unbearable sadness—and in Bob Dillweed's case, hostile defiance. Smith slipped his Celebrity Solutions badge into his pocket. He wanted to be friendly—he didn't know how not to be friendly—but he felt embarrassed smiling at these people, even though he didn't know how not to smile. "How's everybody doing?" was all he could think of saying.

"They tell us we'll go directly to the Cloud," Lady GooGoo said.

"To be with Big Data," added Pelvis Wrestly. "And yet"—he pointed to Kam Kardashiam, sobbing on a bench in a back corner—"some have lost their faith."

"All of us are asking," Beyondée said, "Why me? Why have I been singled out to be dropped from the news feed?"

"I'm not asking that," Bob Dillweed declared. "I'm here because I'm a rebel. The System can't stand rebels."

Smith stared back at him curiously. The System? What was he talking about? All there was in Google Earth was Google and its subsidiaries; in the Cloud there was Big Data and Barney Google. Where was this System he was talking about?

"It didn't have to be this way," Bob Dillweed went on. "I followed the rules so I could be like everybody else, living the Google Earth dream. I went to school for twenty years, but they never put me on the day shift. Instead I ended up here, in the catacombs under the Stadium waiting to be sacrificed."

"I don't understand," Smith mumbled.

"Here's a little song I wrote that tells the story," Bob Dillweed said. He strummed a few chords on the guitar to introduce his song. "I call it 'Substadium Homesick Blues.'"

> *Get born, get shorn,*
> *Get fitted for your uniform*
> *Don't resist, insist*
> *Persist or get pissed*
>
> *Get schooled, re-tooled,*
> *Car-pooled, over-ruled,*
> *Motivated, educated,*
> *Validated, graduated*
>
> *Recruited, rebooted,*
> *Downloaded, decoded,*
> *Unheeded, un-needed,*
> *Defeated, deleted*

Badge in, badge out,
Don't sleep, not a peep,
Take cold showers
Bill your hours

Get time crunched,
Power lunched,
Sunday brunched,
Sucker punched

Abducted, inducted,
Enticed, gene-spliced,
Ready to be sacrificed,
Get costumed, pérfumed,
Faked up, maked-up,
You're on your way to Paradise!

When he heard Bob Dillweed's harsh, nasal singing, Smith understood why he'd been selected for sacrifice. Still, there was something appealing about the man, a sincerity and intensity that made him different from anyone Smith knew. He projected something—there was no word for it, it was an impossible concept, probably connected with his being a "rebel," whatever that meant. He seemed to be saying there were things he didn't *like*—even about his own life. But how could he have a Fakebook page (and everyone had to have a Fakebook page) unless he *liked everything?* Anyone could post cute pictures of his pets—Smith had just added a candid shot of Mot and Derf swimming around their little tank—and almost anyone (even Bosworth) could upload exotic vacation photos attesting to a full, vibrant and exciting life (although in Bosworth's case, Smith, who wasn't one of his friends, knew

that all he did was play video games). So how could it be that
Bob Dillweed would actually *sing* about how dissatisfied he
was? Not only about his own life as a Celebrity about to be
sacrificed, but about Google Earth in general?

As Smith pondered these questions, he could feel one of
his headaches coming on. Meeting the Celebrities had only
added to the anxieties triggered by his dinner with Julia and
O'Brien's strange behavior. Contrary to what he'd always
been told—that Celebrities love being thrown to the lions—
he realized now that they viewed this ritual with fear, loathing
and bitterness. And for the first time he found himself
looking at things from the Celebrities' point of view.
Contemptible as they were, it was understandable that they
didn't want to be torn apart and devoured by wild beasts. Yet
surely, he thought, this must be exactly what Big Data
wanted—Celebrity sacrifices had been going on as long as
anyone could remember. Big Data knows everything, and
controls everything. But since Big Data is the source of
everything that is good in Google Earth, how could Big Data
allow such cruel practices to go on?

Struggling with these questions made Smith break into a
sweat for the first time in his life. He decided to seek counsel
from his personal trainer and spiritual advisor, Reverend
Sidebottom.

10.

As required under the Terms of Service, Smith was a member of the Holy Universal and Infallible Church of Google®, which was the only church in Google Earth. He paid his monthly dues, attended online services, and donated a modest share of his data units to support activities such as bingo, Easter egg hunts and cartoon discussion groups. He'd made no effort to understand the Church's complex theology (having been warned by Customer Service that any attempt to do so would violate the Terms of Service), but its optimistic message—that everyone could be saved—persuaded him that even his recent doubts and anxieties could be overcome. He hoped that a meeting with Reverend Sidebottom would restore the cheerful if mindless outlook on life he'd enjoyed as long as he could remember.

Reverend Sidebottom himself was the picture of mental and physical health. He welcomed Smith at the Church entrance and led him into his office, which was furnished like a luxury condo. As in any condo, one wall was a screen and one was recessed to form a kitchen. The other two walls were picture windows looking into the sanctuary (sometimes called the "gym"), a large open room full of hulking metal frames fitted up with wires, pulleys and weights, which resembled medieval torture devices. Some of the parishioners were entangled in these contraptions, while others tried to escape on exit ramps that carried them back at the same speed as they advanced, giving them the appearance of running in place, or by struggling to pedal away on bikes that were locked to the floor. A pair of beautiful women (all women in Google Earth were beautiful, as Smith had just begun to appreciate), dressed in tight-fitting outfits that emphasized their bulges and curves, glided by the picture windows on their way to the showers. They waved to Reverend Sidebottom, and he waved back at them, his eyes gleaming with the same light Smith had noticed in O'Brien's eyes the day before. "Good session, ladies!" he called out as the women passed the door. "Tomorrow let's work on those abs!"

Loud music pulsed through the office and the sanctuary: a familiar tune that Smith remembered hearing at one of the recent sacrifices. Reverend Sidebottom pointed at a music menu on his screen. "What would you like to hear? Pelvis Wrestly? The Bleach Boys? The Jackman Five?"

Smith requested a Vietnamese hip-hop single he'd discovered recently on iTunes: "Yo Wazup Ho Lady," by Doo-Wop Diggly Scoop Dog XXVI.

"We only play the oldies here," the Reverend sniffed. "After all, this is a church."

Reverend Sidebottom wore traditional clerical garb—a purple thong and a gray hoodie over a pink silk wife-beater. He glanced at his gold watch and hurried toward the kitchen. "I'm afraid the time is getting away from me," he told Smith. "I've got a busload of Beast Folk coming in for Pilates class in half an hour, and I've got to eat lunch first. Would you care to join me?"

Opening the refrigerator, he took out a loaf of bread, some fresh tomatoes and a bowl of eggs, which he set on the table in front of Smith.

"No, I couldn't," Smith hesitated, and not just out of politeness: the tomato looked suspiciously round, as if it might have been plucked off an organic tomato plant, and the eggs—there was no telling where the eggs had come from.

"Don't worry," the Reverend tittered. "It's all strictly GMO. Watch this!" He grabbed one of the tomatoes and hurled it against the screen with all his might.

Smith was relieved to see that instead of exploding it bounced back into the Reverend's hand like a tennis ball. "OK," he said, "I'll try a tomato. But what about the eggs? I mean—"

"The eggs came from Whole Foods, with a chicken lifestyle guarantee. Here, let me play it for you."

Reverend Sidebottom pointed his remote at the serial number on one of the eggs and activated the informational video that came with it, showing the inside of a spacious condo decorated with tasteful Scandinavian furniture and framed barnyard scenes. A solitary hen roosted in a comfortable nest set into a modular shelf. "Satisfied?" the Reverend asked.

"That chicken's condo is bigger than mine!"

"Well, naturally. It's a regulation free-ranging chicken. Private condo, minimum 500 square feet."

"I'm free-ranging too," Smith objected, "and my condo's only 400 square feet."

Rev. Sidebottom lowered his eyes in embarrassment. "And what was it you wanted to talk to me about?" he asked, peeling one of the eggs.

So far the conversation had done nothing for Smith but give him a headache. He was glad it had finally come around to the purpose of his visit. "I've been feeling sort of troubled lately," he began. "At the office, mainly. I do publicity for Celebrity Solutions."

"Ah, yes!" the Reverend beamed. "Any good sacrifices coming up? I've been *so* looking forward to seeing Scarlatina Johnnson getting tossed into the ring!"

"I don't know," Smith said. "I'm starting to feel like maybe there should be a better way to treat the Celebrities. I mean—"

"Celebrities *love* to be sacrificed," Rev. Sidebottom insisted. "It's the role of a lifetime. And besides, it's only their bodies that get devoured by the lions. Their data goes straight to the Cloud, to be with Big Data. What more could anyone ask?"

Now we're getting somewhere, Smith thought. Maybe there was something in the Church's teachings that could help him deal with his fears about termination of service. "That's something I've always wondered about," he said. "Is the Cloud in Big Data, or is Big Data in the Cloud?"

The Reverend sprinkled salt and pepper on his egg and popped it whole into his mouth. "Ah," he sighed. "Men more learned than I have pondered that question for centuries without finding an answer."

"And which came first: Big Data or the Cloud?"

"That one I can answer: *In the beginning was the Cloud, and the Cloud was with Big Data, and the Cloud was Big Data.* That's scripture."

Smith felt his head throbbing as he tried to understand what the Reverend had said. He thought of Julia. "I have a friend who says Big Data doesn't exist."

"Doesn't exist? That's absurd! Big Data is a perfect being. How could there be a perfect being that doesn't exist?"

"Well—"

"Look around Google Earth, and what do you see? Everything being regulated to perfection by a master algorithm. How could that be, if Big Data didn't exist?"

"My friend says Big Data is just a computer somewhere."

"A computer?" the Reverend scoffed. "No, most decidedly not! Big Data may manifest itself through a computer but it is not a computer and it is not *in* a computer."

As if in need of fortification before wading further into theology, Rev. Sidebottom jumped back into the kitchen and returned with a bottle of white wine and a wine glass. He poured himself a glass of wine (without offering any to Smith) and peeled another egg. Then he sliced the tomato he had thrown at the wall and built himself a sandwich of sliced tomato and egg. "Unlike a computer," he said, "Big Data— any data—is not a human invention. A computer is a data processor, so data must have existed before computers were invented. It follows that data can and does exist outside of computers. And that stands to reason, for how can data, which is immaterial in nature, reside in a computer, which is nothing but metal and plastic? Being immaterial, data does not occupy space, so it would be absurd to say that it is located inside a computer. And since that is true even of ordinary data, how much more powerfully true must it be of

Big Data, the fullest, most perfect, most accurate data in the cosmos! It follows (as if proof were necessary) that your friend is wrong. Big Data is not a computer and it is not *in* a computer."

"Where is Big Data, then?"

"Big Data is in the Cloud."

"*What* is Big Data?"

"All we can know about Big Data is that it's not us. Where we are, Big Data is not. Where Big Data is, we are not. *What* Big Data is, we are not. That's all we know and all we'll ever know."

"Then what are *we?*"

"To the extent that we are data—and that's essentially what we are, as the Church teaches—we are also immaterial and outside of space and time. Thus our existence is not bounded by Google Earth. Upon termination of service—which is defined in the Terms of Service as the date on which one's data is abstracted from the physical body—we may or may not be saved to the Cloud, to be incorporated into Big Data."

The music blaring from the speakers had stopped. Rev. Sidebottom took a moment to select another album from his music menu. "Do you like Smoky Robinson and the Miracles?" he asked. "Or how about Credence Clearwater Revival?"

Smith waved these questions aside as he wrestled, for the first time, with what he later learned was existential angst. "If I'm not saved," he asked, "where will I go? Would I just... vanish?"

"That depends on how you've lived your life," the Reverend said, taking a generous bite from his sandwich.

"Did you comply with all relevant Google policies, including policies relating to diversity, bullying and record retention? Did you complete all required compliance training? Did you fulfill your obligations under the Terms of Service? In short, is there anything about you that's worth saving?"

"I was hoping that just believing in the right things—believing in Barney Google, for instance, and liking the right TV shows, and being polite to Customer Service—"

"Those things are important, but by themselves they're not enough."

"But don't we get a second chance?   I mean, some people get transferred to Omaha—"

"Have you ever been to Omaha?"

"No, but—"

"Trust me, you don't want to go there." The Reverend poured himself a second glass of wine and went on: "I'll say this, though, if you think you might have reason to worry. You can avoid going to Omaha if you make a generous contribution to the Church. We can put a word in for you in the Cloud."

Smith was incredulous. "You communicate directly with Big Data?"

"Not directly," Reverend Sidebottom conceded. "No one can do that. But we've kept lines of communication open with certain Celebrities who've gone up there."

"Like who, for instance?"

"Do you remember Peter, Paul and Mary?"

11

Higgs could think about nothing but the Next Big Thing. Ralph was supportive, but certain formalities—including approval by the Board of Directors—had to be observed. The trick would be not telling the Board what the Next Big Thing actually was. Luckily, under the by-laws only the marketing slogan required Board approval.

To address these concerns, Higgs convened an emergency meeting of the Board of Directors, in the form of a video conference. "Big Data is watching you!" he declaimed, raising his hand in the Google salute. "Big Data is watching you!" the other three Directors saluted. Their names were Bumstead, Chang and Eng. Bumstead was an amiable nerd (at Google, to be called a nerd was the highest praise) who had spent many years in Customer Service. Chang and Eng were refugees from Walt Disney World who'd been elected to the Board for diversity reasons. They represented a minority group—Siamese twins of opposite gender—consisting only of themselves. However, they made ideal Directors since their presence at a meeting along with Higgs constituted a quorum.

"I organized this Board meeting to brief you about our latest initiative," Higgs began. "I call it the 'Next Big Thing.'" He flashed a PowerPoint slide on the screen. "Why do I call it the 'Next Big Thing?' Let me break that down for you."

Higgs highlighted the first of three bullet points on the slide. "First, I call it 'Next' because it's an expedited item on the calendar for the near future. Secondly, it's 'Big' because it's literally earth-shaking in its implications. And thirdly, it's a 'Thing' because"—he ducked his head and rasped into his EyeWatch: "Why is it a 'thing?'"

"Everything is a thing," Ralph whispered.

"Right." Higgs leveled his gaze at the three Directors on the screen with the no-nonsense air of authority that was part of his brand. "It's a 'thing' because, quite frankly, everything is a thing."

In past meetings Bumstead had earned a reputation as the Board skeptic. "Could you be a little more specific?" he asked.

"Certainement. Let's focus on the marketing slogan. I'm going to suggest *Fulfilling Our Biological Destiny.*"

"That sounds good," Chang and Eng said in unison.

"But what's *biological* about it?" Bumstead wanted to know.

"Nothing, really," Higgs said, "at the end of the day."

"And it really will be the end of the day," Ralph gloated. "Lights out!"

The Directors seemed alarmed at Ralph's intrusion. "Is someone else on the line?" Bumstead asked.

"It's OK," Higgs explained. "It's just my EyeWatch with the Microsoft YesMan™ app. I call him Ralph."

The Directors sighed in relief and Higgs went on: "I agree that biology may not be the right theme. How about shortening the slogan to *Fulfilling Our Destiny?*"

"Shouldn't there be some reference...," Chang began, and Eng completed the thought, "to Big Data or the Cloud?"

"Yes," Bumstead jumped in. "'Destiny' sounds too ominous. Shouldn't we paint the future in a more positive light?"

"Those are all excellent points," Higgs said, smiling broadly. "I think I've got it: *Find Your Future in the Cloud.*"

"That's perfect," Chang beamed.

"That's perfect," Eng beamed.

"We're all in agreement, then?" Higgs asked. "The Next Big Thing is approved?"

"Yes!" Chang shouted, nodding enthusiastically.

"Yes!" Eng shouted, nodding enthusiastically.

The Siamese twins nodded so enthusiastically that they bumped heads and disappeared off the screen. "I'm afraid we've lost our quorum," Higgs said, turning his gaze on Bumstead. "Do I have your vote?"

The skeptical Bumstead seemed to relish his sudden access of power. "I'd like to hear Ralph's perspective," he said.

Thirty minutes later, Higgs stepped onto the balcony to enjoy his view of the Sea of Shells and congratulate himself on a job well done. He'd had his way with the Board, but he knew better than to let this success go to his head. Board approval was only the first of many obstacles he'd have to overcome. The devil, as always, was in the details. "The Next Big Thing has been approved," he mused. "The only question now is how to bring it off."

"I'm thinking Jonestown," Ralph said.

O'Brien was expected momentarily. Higgs readied the bedroom for her visit, stripping the bed and remaking it with red satin sheets and pillowcases. He drew the curtains and adjusted the lighting so that it was soft and sensuous but not too dim. Then he tidied up the living room, dusting his collection of antique remote controls and Barney Google bobble heads. As Higgs went about these tasks, Ralph glowed with quiet pride at the important role he'd played in the Board meeting. After Chang and Eng had passed out and Bumstead voiced his misgivings about the slogan *Find Your Future In The Cloud,* it was Ralph who, through subtle threats involving a possible transfer to Omaha, had persuaded Bumstead to abstain, and then had cast the deciding vote. Not that Ralph could count on the recognition he deserved. Higgs, in his self-importance, seemed oblivious to his assistant's contributions. He forgot all about Ralph, congratulating himself about the Board approval, even the Jonestown idea, as if Ralph wasn't even there. And when O'Brien arrived—in an omission that would have far-reaching consequences—he forgot to remove his EyeWatch.

After a few minutes of small talk, Higgs grabbed O'Brien's hand and pulled her into the bedroom. While she made herself comfortable, he slipped into his home office— which was his only office—to dispatch a quick message to Advertising about the new slogan. If Higgs had a weakness as CEO, it was in the area of work/life balance. Even when he was with one of his mistresses from the Junior Anti-Sex League, he couldn't keep his mind off business—or stop talking about it—for more than a few seconds. However, he flattered himself that his work ethic didn't detract from his mistresses' satisfaction. To that end, as he dashed off his message to Advertising, he fantasized about O'Brien waiting for him in the bedroom.

His message sent, he threw off his clothes and rushed back into the bedroom, where O'Brien lay stretched out on the bed, partially draped in a satin sheet. "Are you ready for the Next Big Thing?" he asked her.

Her eyes widened. "Am I ever!"

"It's been approved by the Board of Directors."

She gasped. "You've shown it to them too?"

"The problem is," he nodded, "I'm not sure if a certain member"—he was thinking of Bumstead—"can be trusted to do his job."

"Looks like a stand-up guy to me!"

Higgs stretched out beside her and quickly got down to the matter at hand—too quickly, O'Brien thought, though she didn't complain. It was the continuing monologue that she found annoying, a rehash of the Board meeting and his plans for the new project. The only thing missing was PowerPoint slides. He rambled on about the Next Big Thing, the approved slogan, his need for support from Celebrity Solutions—"Because, don't you see? it's really just a Celebrity sacrifice on a grand scale!"—and his suspicion that Bumstead was in league with Goldstein. She had no idea what he was talking about, and under the circumstances she couldn't have cared less, although, as she thought about it later, she should have been alarmed at the maniacal gleam in his eyes. She tried to block the monologue by focusing her mind on other things: oddly, she fantasized about Smith, who seemed to have undergone an awakening in recent days like the one she'd experienced after her first visit to the penthouse. Had Smith found a way to dodge the anti-sex waves? She found him increasingly attractive. Higgs, for all his wealth and power, was cold and calculating, consumed by his obsession with his job. Even his caresses seemed to be arranged in bullet points.

Higgs sensed that his monologue had dampened O'Brien's enthusiasm. Recalling their last encounter, he started murmuring the names of non-GMO foods in her ear. This tactic had the desired effect of triggering the continuous affirmative consent required by Google sex policy.

"Yes!" O'Brien cried out. Her breathing quickened, her eyes glazed over, and at the mention of Philly cheese steaks a tsunami of forbidden food associations swept over her and carried her away. "Yes!" she shouted again. "Yes!"

"Yes," Ralph agreed.

With a gasp she rolled away from Higgs and pulled the satin sheet over her head. "Is somebody in here?"

"It's only Ralph!" Higgs laughed, holding up his EyeWatch. "Just think of him as a eunuch guarding the harem."

"Precisely," Ralph agreed. But Higgs's words, reverberating through his circuits, stung like a bully's slap. Being called a eunuch was an insult he would not soon forget.

O'Brien poked her blushing face out from under the covers. "You're not filming this, are you?" she asked Higgs.

"Don't be ridiculous!"

12.

Smith sat in his cubicle, thinking about Julia. He'd been thinking about her incessantly for the past few days, without knowing why. He liked her, of course, but so what? You couldn't not like somebody. For some reason she seemed special—and that, he sensed, was a thought he should keep to himself. The only people you were supposed to feel that way about were your pets. Julia, even if she turned out to be a hominid, would never be approved as a pet by the Condominium Homeowners Association. Unlike Mot and Derf, she might make noise that would disturb the neighbors. There was no room for her in his unit—where would she sleep?—and he couldn't afford to feed her the kind of food she needed (if they even carried hominid food at Petco). In any event, he felt differently about Julia than he felt about Mot and Derf. There must have been something else going on, something connected with that dinner she had served him.

All in all it had been a difficult week. Besides the obsession with Julia, he'd been troubled by his sudden fascination with O'Brien, especially her breasts, but to a lesser extent her hips and her exquisitely narrow waist. Then there had been his disturbing visit to the Celebrities and the unfamiliar emotions it aroused, followed by his discussion with Rev. Sidebottom, which had left him feeling like a temporary data configuration, unlikely ever to be saved to the

Cloud. And that morning, as his toothbrush cleaned his teeth, he'd noticed something even more upsetting: there were little hairs growing out of his face. Thousands of them, peeping out of every pore, casting a dark shadow where his happy face had beamed brightly for as long as he could remember. And when, arriving at the office, he passed Bosworth's work station (where Bosworth sat entranced by his video games) and greeted him with "Big Data is watching you!," his voice seemed to separate into halves, one normally high and the other abnormally, almost bestially low, as if a bone had caught in his throat. Bosworth smirked and turned away, driving Smith to hide in his cubicle for the rest of the morning. Luckily, O'Brien was not in the office, having stopped on the way in (her secretary said) for an important meeting with Higgs.

At lunchtime Smith's car drove him to McDonalds, the quick nourishment restaurant. Quick nourishment was a major advance over traditional GMO foods such as Greek yogurt, granola and arugula. Its manufacturer, Monsanto, used a patented process to eliminate needless fillers, compressing the genetically modified nutrients themselves— proteins, carbohydrates, enzymes, vitamins—into brightly colored tablets shaped like popular cartoon characters. The best thing about quick nourishment, in Smith's opinion, was that it had no taste, apart from a vague aura of citrus that reminded him of Kool Aid. (The elimination of taste from food had been noticed only by a few snobs of questionable brand loyalty who had been sent to customer re-education camps near Omaha.) Since Smith's car was sponsored by McDonalds, it took him to the McDonalds drive-up window twice a day, where he was greeted by the friendly voice of Big

Mackie, the CEO of McDonalds. He rarely ventured out of his car at McDonalds. Renegade bands of glue-sniffing Yoots roamed the parking lot, muttering incoherently as they watched YootTube videos on their phones. Inside the restaurant, the cooks, cashiers and clean-up crew were Beast Folk who concentrated more on the pulse in their ear pods than on the desires of the customers. When they spoke, it was in an unintelligible Beast Folk dialect.

Smith ordered a Happy Lunch, consisting of a Monsantopatty® (patent pending), a medium order of desiccated carbohydrate cubes, a fountain Kool Aid, and a plastic replica of one of his favorite cartoon characters. "Have a great day," Big Mackie's voice said as the Happy Lunch flew out through a chute into his car.

That was what Big Mackie said every day: "Have a great day." It was what Big Mackie had said every day for as long as Smith could remember. But today, he sensed, Big Mackie's tone sounded different: a little ironic, almost mocking. It was almost as if—he dismissed the thought as soon as it entered his mind—Big Mackie didn't really want him to have a great day. That's ridiculous, he told himself. Of course I'll have a great day. What other kind of day could there be? But even asking the question made him uncomfortable. Somewhere in his mind the seeds of doubt had been planted.

He spent a grueling afternoon composing tweets for the upcoming sacrifice, which would feature Justin Bleeper and Smiley Cirrus. When he finished the tweets, he dropped them off at the Message Center with instructions on when to send them out. Most of the actual work in the Message Center was performed by Interns indentured to Celebrity

Solutions while they repaid their student loans. Theoretically this was for a limited time—until the loans were paid off—but since Celebrity Solutions didn't pay the Interns (instead giving them valuable work experience), and interest continued to accrue on the loans, the practical length of the internships was perpetual. Some people joked about unpaid Interns who worked there hundreds of years and then were sent to Omaha before landing their first real job. Still, the perky and eager-to-please interns were preferable to the sullen Beast Folk who sometimes filled in during the summer months. When Smith arrived that afternoon he was greeted by a perky Intern named McClellan, whom he immediately identified as a woman. She was shaped just like Julia, which was reassuring, because he knew that the Message Center would never hire hominids, even as Interns.

"Big Data is watching you!" McClellan said, her eyes gleaming. "Can I help you with something?"

He could tell that she was staring at the little hairs on his face. "Here!" he said sharply. He hoped to distract her by speaking with an authoritative air—"Send out these two tweets tomorrow at exactly ten o'clock!"—but the spell was broken when his voice split into two octaves, and sweat, for the first time in his life, poured out of his underarms.

"For you," she beamed, "I'd do just about anything."

He turned on his heels and fled back to his desk, only to find O'Brien lurking in the next cubicle. Her eyes, like McClellan's, appeared to be gleaming—though not, he assumed, in the hope of being released from perpetual durance as an Intern. He had no way of knowing that O'Brien had just returned from her frustrating date with

Higgs and (as it turned out) Ralph, who had spoken up at just the wrong moment.

"Looks like you need a shave, handsome," O'Brien cooed.

"What?"

"You're so innocent!"

He had no clue what she was talking about. All he knew was that women—now that he'd suddenly started noticing them—were driving him to distraction. He needed to take *It's A Wonderful Life* back to Charrington's, and that gave him an idea. He'd see if he could rent a movie that would teach him more about women, maybe one of the titles Julia had recommended. Maybe then he could understand what was going on.

Smith left work early, stopping as usual at McDonalds for a Happy Dinner (identical to his Happy Lunch except for the toy, which was a tiny replica of Foghorn Leghorn). The sun was still well above the horizon when his car parked itself near the old deserted mall where Charrington's Antiques was located. He picked his way through the weeds and brush that clogged the ancient parking lot, ducking behind a Barney Google statue when the Customer Service van cruised by. Again he used the casual approach, slipping into the shop as if on impulse; again Charrington slouched behind the counter, watching sacrifices on his screen. Smith feigned interest in the antiques—an early EyePhone, a framed portrait of Darnold Grump before he went to prison, the "I Like Ike" poster he'd noticed on his first visit—even though, in his opinion, they were nothing but junk.

"That's a real collector's item," Charrington said without turning around, referring to the "I Like Ike" poster. "You won't find another one like it in that condition."

Smith wandered through a turnstile into the Collectors Only section, where Charrington kept the racier items such as back issues of *Orgasmic Gardening* and *Martha Stewart Life,* wrapped in cellophane to keep the Beast Folk from peeking inside them. He quickly turned around and came back through the turnstile, so Charrington wouldn't think he had come in to look at dirty magazines. He was there to return *It's A Wonderful Life.* "Here," he said, stepping up to the counter. "I need to return this."

"Disgusting, isn't it?" Charrington asked, shoving the movie under the counter. "Well, what did you expect?"

Smith lowered his voice, even though he hadn't noticed anyone else in the shop. "I was wondering if you might have some more recent hominid movies," he said. "One with better pictures of women's breasts."

"Just their breasts?"

"It's for a study I'm doing. An educational study. A friend of mine suggested *Debby Does Dubai.*"

Charrington squinted at him warily. *"Debby Does Dubai* is out, I'm afraid." He groped under the counter and shoved something into a brown plastic bag. "But I've got just the thing for you: *Topless Meteorologists Do Action News.* Just came in today. Even includes a weather report."

Smith hesitated as he tried to remember the name of the other movie Julia had recommended. "All right."

Charrington smiled for the first time. "It'll be quite an education for you."

13.

Smith had a spring in his step when he arrived at the condo, looking forward to an evening of illicit movie viewing. He finished what was left of his Happy Dinner, adding his new toys to the display case on the windowsill. Then, in the bathroom, he noticed with alarm that the little hairs on his face had grown darker and thicker, giving him an unsavory, primitive appearance, almost like a hominid. He scrubbed his face with soap and water, but that only made the little hairs stand out more. Anxious to start having fun, he drew the curtains, popped some popcorn, and settled back in his easy chair to watch *Topless Meteorologists Do Action News*.

The instant the movie flashed on his screen he knew something was seriously wrong. Instead of scantily-clad meteorologists beaming at weather maps, he saw a gang of brutish men in black uniforms carrying submachine guns, their faces concealed under masks that looked like black pillow cases with eye-holes. The men wore "I Like Ike" buttons on their uniforms, and an enormous "I Like Ike" poster filled the wall behind them. But in place of the genial bald man on the poster at the antique shop, this one showed the hideous face of Goldstein. Everyone knew that face—the insidious smile, the combed-back white hair, the black eyebrows beetling over dark, deeply-recessed eyes—but few had seen it displayed so brazenly. Isaac "Ike" Goldstein was the embodiment of everything destructive and hateful, the unraveler of the social network, the Anti-Google. As long as Smith could remember, there had been denunciations and warnings in the news feed about Goldstein and his subversive brotherhood, known as the Resistance. But what in Google Earth did Goldstein have to do with meteorologists? The only thing Smith could think of was that Charrington had mistakenly slipped this Goldstein video into his bag instead of the one he'd mentioned. But no, there was another movie in the bag. Charrington had given him two movies and he'd just happened to pull this one out first.

Now Goldstein's real face filled the screen. It was no less hideous than his picture, though admittedly more human. He stretched it into a smile and said in a surprisingly gentle tone: *"Big Data is watching you!"*

That was the traditional salutation, of course. Smith was astonished to hear it coming from a man who had sworn to destroy Big Data.

"How many times have you uttered that greeting?" Goldstein continued. "To start the day with a co-worker. To open a meeting. To initiate a conversation with Customer Service. We've all said it so many times we hardly know what it means anymore. Most people, if they think about that phrase at all, take comfort in the security it implies: Big Data will watch over you, protect you, provide for your needs."

The camera had gradually zoomed out, away from Goldstein's face until he could be seen at full length on a stage addressing an invisible audience. He wore a black uniform and was flanked by guards carrying submachine guns. An "I Like Ike" poster filled the wall behind him.

Goldstein smiled amiably at the audience and introduced himself: "My name is Ike Goldstein," he said. "You probably think you know all about me. You also probably think you know all about Big Data. Well, I'm here to tell you that everything you think you know about Big Data is a *lie*. And every slogan you've been made to memorize is *false:*

"*Freedom is not connectivity*. It is the opposite: it is independence.

"*Choice is not obedience*. It is the opposite: it is rebellion.

"*Privacy is not sharing*. It is the opposite: it is secrecy."

Sounds of unrest could be heard coming from the audience. A buzz of resistance or agreement. Some hissing, a few catcalls and shouts. The guards stepped closer to Goldstein and aimed threatening glances at the audience.

Goldstein waited for the crowd to settle down and went on: "Before I proceed," he said, "I have to admit that I just told you a fib, for which I hope you'll forgive me. There is one slogan you've been made to memorize—the one I began with today—that isn't false. Big Data really is watching you!"

Nervous tittering from the audience. "Please bear with me," Goldstein smiled. "I'm going to say some things that will probably shock you. And at the end of this speech I'm going to tell you the truth about something else you've been lied to about all your life. I'm going to reveal the *Big Secret* that Google doesn't want you to know."

Smith didn't have to wait until the end to be shocked by Goldstein's speech. He sat writhing in his chair, hurling handfuls of popcorn at the screen. It was the closest he'd ever come to being infuriated. Why should he listen to this nonsense? No one is allowed to say these things! On the other hand (an inner voice whispered), there was Goldstein—

on the screen—saying these things that couldn't be said. You have to believe what you see on a screen; that had always been the rule, so far as Smith knew. But did it apply to things that couldn't be said? The issues were too complicated to be sorted out with the number of data units in Smith's allotment. Maybe, he thought, he should keep watching the speech a few minutes longer, just to see how ridiculous it was.

Goldstein was talking, in a more earnest voice, about something called the Internet. "In the beginning," he said, "the Internet was the embodiment of human freedom. You could go anywhere on it, say anything, find anything. Incredible as it may seem today, everyone had a connection to it in their home and even on their phone. What began as a chain of computers grew into a worldwide web, collecting and linking so much data that there was no longer any excuse for disease, death, conflict or unhappiness. But as we soon learned, that world of connectivity also had no room for privacy, freedom or choice. The promise of Big Data was too powerful for the Internet to remain an instrument of freedom. It was as if the web had been spun by a deadly spider and baited with the temptation of perfect knowledge, that would make men gods—and when the snare was tripped, it folded around its prey at a dizzying speed. The dream of perfect knowledge became a nightmare of perpetual control. And in case you think this is just a fairy tale—if you're asking, does this worldwide web still exist?—my answer is Yes, of course it still exists, but you no longer have access to it. You used to search the Internet; now it searches *you.*"

This last part made Smith uncomfortable. Sometimes as he lay in bed at night he imagined that he could feel WiFi waves beaming down on him from the nearby tower, just as

Julia's Uncle Floyd had claimed. For all he knew, those waves tinkered with his body and even with his mind as he slept, which would explain, for one thing, why he always felt so much better when he woke up. He had taken Uncle Floyd for a Yahoo crackpot, and even wondered if he was somehow mixed up with Goldstein, which now seemed highly likely. But some of his ideas were starting to make sense in light of what Goldstein had said. How could privacy be sharing? How could obedience be choice? And why would Julia and the others in Coolidgeville (assuming they weren't hominids) be so different from everyone else, if not for the tin pie plate blocking transmissions from the local tower, as Uncle Floyd had claimed?

"Now," Goldstein said, "you're probably wondering: How did this situation come about? How did we get where we are today?"

No, he had not been wondering that at all, Smith muttered. It had never occurred to him to wonder about the past, any more than he wondered about the future. The past only went back thirty days, and the future couldn't go any farther forward than the past went backwards. Why would anybody be interested in either of those things?

"I won't attempt to describe the disasters that befell the human race starting about four hundred years ago," Goldstein went on. "I'll just say this: In the wake of those disasters, one company survived and prospered: Google. The world's money was gone, but Google had something far more valuable than money: it had data, an enormous store of data and the algorithms to use it. Google traded rights in this data for the stock of all the companies on the stock exchange and closed all the banks in order to make sure that money would never be used again. To the surviving members of the public, who had lost all their money, Google said: Don't worry! You don't need money. You've got data—or rather, *we've* got data—and that's all you're ever going to need. The money economy was replaced by the data unit system we use today. The days of wage slavery were over.

"In those days there was also something called the government, which has since withered away. The government was the remnant of a primitive custom dating back to prehistoric times, under which groups of men with a monopoly on violence ruled over society and everyone else obeyed their commands. After the money collapse and the Great Stench, Google convinced the public that the government no longer served a purpose. With enough data, they proclaimed, human life could be free of coercion and yet be perfectly regulated.

"Thus Google offered an alternative to two hated institutions, the economy and the government. But in a few short years it became far more oppressive than either of them had ever been. People looked back fondly on the inefficiency and waste of the economy—even *losing* all your money seemed better than never having it at all. And the government's monopoly on violence had been nothing compared to Google's monopoly on data. Government at least had the virtue of ignorance and stupidity. There was a limit to the harm it could do as long as its access to information was limited. Google worked under no such constraint. It set its goal as knowing *everything* about the customers it "served"—but the more Google knew about them, the more they served Google, not the other way around. As the data set expanded and the algorithms improved, the customers became little more than slaves. The Terms of Service were secretly amended to become Terms of Servitude."

Smith leaped out of his chair and pushed the remote control to split his screen into halves. At last he had a hard, objective fact that he could check: Goldstein's claim that the Terms of Service had been changed to Terms of Servitude. If that claim was false, then Goldstein's convoluted attack on Google (so absurd that it hardly needed to be disproved) fell apart. Smith had conscientiously adhered to the Terms of Service every day of his life. Never before had anyone suggested that they had changed into Terms of Servitude. The Google home page lit up its half of the screen. Smith found the word "Terms," clicked on an icon that looked surprisingly like a pair of handcuffs, and waited for the Terms of Service to appear. Instead, a bucolic scene rose before him, with a legend advising him that the page he requested was temporarily out of service. How can the Terms of Service be out of service? he asked himself. Even temporarily! That would be like saying Gravity™ was temporarily out of service!

"External surveillance," Goldstein droned on, "which had been controversial when it began, became unnecessary when internal surveillance—within the human body—was perfected. At first this was aimed at medical improvements, such as monitoring blood sugar or cholesterol. It expanded from there to the endocrine system, the immune system, the gonads and sex hormones, and then to neural transmitters and genetic modification, with hundreds of cookies, pixel tags and nano-sensors located in each person's body monitoring and transmitting data to and from Google's servers, and hundreds of similar nano-devices to make the necessary adjustments (all running on software copyrighted by Google). Cancer, heart disease, schizophrenia, diabetes, aging itself— all were cured. Before long the nanobots became self-repairing, self-improving and self-replicating. In the space of a few years, mankind's fondest dreams—perfect health and immortality—had been achieved."

Goldstein stopped talking and smiled as if he wanted to share a little joke with the audience. "I should mention, just as an aside, that there was one segment of the population that resisted these improvements. These were the young people known in those days as teenagers. Today we call them the Beast Folk. They were just as beastly then as they are now, and shutting down their gonads proved a monumental task. Eventually they were pacified with drugs, music and phones, especially phones. Even today, Google recognizes that it could never control the Beast Folk without the YootTube videos that are constantly streamed to their phones. Since aging has been eliminated, the Beast Folk have become a permanent caste, assigned either to food service or to membership in the Yoots, an elite army of thugs protecting Senior Management. Once a proud, defiant market segment, the Beast Folk's message allotments have steadily dwindled, until today you seldom hear them grunt more than a few garbled syllables."

Smith pressed the remote to stop the video. On the other half of the screen, he clicked on the handcuffs icon, still intent on reading the Terms of Service. Again he got the bucolic scene and the "Temporarily Out of Service" message. All he could do was keep trying, he decided. Surely the Terms of Service would be available soon.

14.

Smith felt more keenly than ever the need to find hard proof debunking Goldstein's heresies. Without such proof, he realized, he might be misled by their superficial glamour and appeal. It was hard, almost impossible, not to believe anything he saw on a screen, even (and this thought surprised him) if he didn't really believe it. If he'd stumbled on this movie two weeks ago, he would have clicked it off after five seconds and dismissed it from his mind. But since meeting Julia he'd felt confused, troubled and open to temptation, though he still didn't understand what temptation was. Apprehensively, he rubbed his chin and confirmed that the little hairs had grown. Those hairs were somehow connected with his new receptiveness to subversive ideas, as if they were tiny WiFi antennas receiving signals from a different tower.

"In addition to physical perfection," Goldstein was saying, "Google had an even greater prize within its grasp: perfect knowledge. The Google servers knew more about each person than that person could ever have known about himself or herself. That knowledge—at first jocularly, then reverently called Big Data—came to be seen as a kind of all-powerful, all-knowing Providence, watching over Google Earth from the Cloud. What started as a business tactic had morphed into a religion. Big Data had become God."

"What is he talking about?" Smith cried aloud. Of course Big Data watched over Google Earth from the Cloud. Was Goldstein even questioning that?

"The fact that this system was based on science," Goldstein went on, "not God or nature, was quickly forgotten. People started believing that life had always been this way and could never be any different. They had no idea of what was going on inside their bodies, or between their bodies and the Google servers."

Smith broke into a cold sweat. His breathing was labored, his eyes wild as he tore them away from the screen and stared at the two pictures on his wall, the same two pictures every condo had on its wall: Big Data—glowing, nebulous, not really human—and Barney Google, its human incarnation, who looked reassuringly like a cartoon character: a little old man in a top hat, like the millionaire in a Monopoly® game. Hadn't Big Data always been in the Cloud? Hadn't Barney Google come down to Google Earth so that everyone's data could be saved?

"Google realized that to maintain its power it would have to control the mind as well as the body," Goldstein said. "Once again Big Data came to the rescue. Based on the law of large numbers, the algorithms could predict with startling accuracy exactly what a person was thinking and what he or she would think next. This 'thought feed' could be relayed to others within a designated range—such as one's co-workers—by stimulating chemical processes in their brains which would trigger parallel thought processes. In this way the last bastion of privacy—the privacy of one's own thoughts—became another form of sharing.

"Google still needed a way to translate this mind-reading into practical control. The Terms of Servitude—draconian as they were—left something to be desired, since no one could understand them. Google found the solution in the Copyright Act. By this time the government had withered to a few shabby offices in what had been Arlington, Virginia. The President (typically a crusty octogenarian from Walt Disney World) functioned like the Town Clerk of a rural Southern town. All that remained of Congress was a small coterie of liars and thieves (down from a much larger coterie in former times) that hung around street corners begging for campaign contributions. Google's subsidiary, the Walt Disney Company, bribed them to vote for a law extending all copyrights in perpetuity. Congress not only passed that amendment but made it apply retroactively to every document Google had ever searched or scanned, including the Oxford English Dictionary. Thus Google obtained a perpetual copyright on virtually every sentence that had ever been written, and on every word and possible combination of words in the English language, for which it promptly filed a trademark application. In this fashion Google became the sole owner of English®. The Terms of Servitude were amended to prohibit the use of any other language, and to license English® users to think and communicate only in certain pre-authorized allotments of data units. Any other use of English® was declared a copyright infringement."

That's it! Smith thought, clicking off the movie. Once again Goldstein had mentioned something—Google's alleged copyright on English® and the ban on other languages—that could be checked for accuracy as soon as the Terms of Service could be accessed. Since the "Temporarily Out of

Service" message was still up, he fast-forwarded to the end of the movie, anxious to hear the Big Secret that had been promised at the beginning.

Goldstein held his fist raised in a kind of salute. "The Resistance is founded on these principles," he proclaimed. "Big Data is not God. The Cloud is not Paradise. The Master Algorithm is not the Law!"

Cheers rose from the audience, and Goldstein went on: "We demand the right to be people again, not valued customers, not trusted partners, not data sets!"

More cheers, shouts, stamping of feet. "We will fight to the death for the freedom of every man and woman to think their own thoughts," Goldstein declared, "unobserved and uninfluenced by Big Data or any other Google activity!"

Goldstein waited for the audience to settle down. Then he lowered his arm and reverted to the relaxed, friendly mode he'd affected at the beginning of his speech. "And the good news is, folks, we don't have to fight a revolution in order to accomplish our goals. The revolution can be won without firing a shot. How?

"At the beginning of this video, I promised to reveal the Big Secret, the one thing Google will go to any length to keep you from knowing. Here it is in a nutshell: *You can do whatever you want!*

"You can be independent! You don't have to obey! You don't have to share!

"You can do whatever you want!"

15.

Smith paused the movie and gaped at Goldstein in astonishment, trying to grasp the Big Secret that had just been revealed. After all the shocking, subversive things Goldstein had said, his fantastic claims about Google, his blasphemy against Big Data and finally his call for a fight to the death (whatever that meant) in the name of freedom, was this what his Big Secret came down to: *"You can do whatever you want"?* Why was that a secret? Smith asked himself. And what was revolutionary about it? He already did exactly what he wanted, which was what Big Data told him to do: that was a free choice, though he had never chosen otherwise, since Big Data knew more about what he wanted than he did. This is what was meant by Obedience Is Choice. Obedience to Big Data was the only rational choice, and therefore only the person who obeys Big Data is truly free. Without connectivity, you wouldn't be able to obey Big Data, and therefore Freedom Is Connectivity. And without sharing, Big Data wouldn't be able to tailor its messages to your personal, private needs, and therefore Privacy Is Sharing. These principles had always been valid, and they always would be. Why all of a sudden did Goldstein think there needed to be a revolution? Smith closed his eyes and cradled his head in his hands. Thinking about these complications made his head ache, as it did when Julia made him read from

the book by Thomas Jefferson. Surely all his questions would
be cleared up as soon as he could read the Terms of Service.

The Google home page suddenly lit up and a friendly
woman's face filled the screen. "I am Mrs. Lopez," the
woman said. "I am your Customer Service Representative.
How can I help you tonight?"

Smith felt his heart pounding. He closed the half of the
screen where Goldstein's smile lingered, hoping the
Customer Service Representative didn't notice what he'd
been watching. "I... didn't call Customer Service," he
stammered.

"No," the woman smiled. "But we noticed that you
made repeated attempts to access the Terms of Service."

Smith breathed a little easier to hear the woman say
"Terms of Service," instead of "Terms of Servitude." It
undermined one of Goldstein's key points and cast a doubtful
light on everything he had said. Smith had learned that the
best way to deal with Customer Service was to be patient and
polite. They're people too, he reminded himself. Mrs.
Lopez—unlike the thugs who'd dropped in to complain
about his TV viewing—wasn't from the enforcement
division. "Thanks," he said. "Yes, I was trying to access the
Terms of Service."

"May I ask why?" Mrs. Lopez asked.

"I just wanted to look something up."

"If you're wondering whether some action you're
contemplating would be a violation, perhaps I can help you?"

"No, it's not that."

"Well," Mrs. Lopez hesitated, "why else would you want
to read the Terms of Service?"

"No particular reason," Smith mumbled. "I just wanted"—he groped for the phrase he'd heard at a training session at the office—"to familiarize myself with them. Aren't the Terms of Service available to everyone?"

"Of course," the representative said pleasantly. "May I remind you that you've already agreed to them? And at that time you represented that you had read and understood them?"

"Not that I had any choice," Smith muttered.

"What did you say?"

"Well, they're the Terms of Service, aren't they? You can't not agree to them."

"That is correct."

"So I had no choice but to agree to them, right? Whether I read and understood them or not."

"I'm afraid I'm going to have to put you on hold," Mrs. Lopez said. "Current waiting time is approximately six hours and thirteen minutes."

Smith couldn't conceal his annoyance. "Six hours? Just to see the Terms of Service?"

The representative's smile faded. "You sound a little desperate to see them, Customer Smith, if you don't mind my saying so."

"How did you know my name?" Smith demanded. "I didn't give you my name."

"Perhaps you should consult our Privacy Policy while you're waiting."

Mrs. Lopez's face was replaced by a swirling screensaver pattern, accompanied by Hold Music. Smith hated Hold Music—frenzied, jangly, alternating between raucous and sickeningly sweet—even more than Mozart, Beethoven and

Brahms. Somewhere in Google Earth there were orchestras spewing out this trash for the sole purpose, he suspected, of making people hang up before their waiting time had elapsed, thus ensuring shorter working hours for Customer Service Representatives. Smith (possibly emboldened by the Goldstein video) refused to yield to this shameless intimidation. He was determined to stay in the queue, even if it took six hours.

To pass the time he touched the icon for *Our Privacy Policy* (which looked surprisingly like a man in a prison cell), as Mrs. Lopez had suggested.

> *Your privacy is important to us* (the Policy read). *That's why we own it and intend to protect it. For this reason we exercise strict control of your data.*

> *Our Privacy Pledge*

> *No one, including you, will ever gain access to your data.*

> *Your data will never be used for any purpose except by Google and its affiliates.*

> *Upon termination of service, your data may be used, stored, deleted or commingled with other data, at the discretion of Google and its affiliates.*

"In other words," Smith said to himself in a sarcastic voice, "Google's privacy policy is that I have no privacy."

"That's not quite true, Customer Smith," Mrs. Lopez said, flashing back onto the screen. "You have a great deal of privacy. It's just that Google owns it." As if to prove her point, she gazed past Smith toward the back wall of his condo. "By the way, that's a nice picture of Angelina Joleen you have on your wall. In your job, do you ever get to meet any of the Celebrities?"

Smith's patience was wearing thin. "How much longer will I have to wait?"

"Current waiting time is approximately eight hours and thirty-seven minutes."

"Eight hours! You said it was six hours before, and that was about an hour ago."

"Waiting times are approximate only. I believe I mentioned that."

"This is ridiculous. Let me talk to your supervisor."

"Current waiting time to speak with a supervisor is approximately eleven hours and sixteen minutes."

Smith stomped around the condo in a rage, overturning his popcorn which he trampled into the rug. "I can't believe this!"

"You would probably not like to speak to my supervisor in any case, sir," Mrs. Lopez said.

"Why not?"

"He will only put you on hold until you ask to speak to his supervisor, who will do the same thing. And each supervisor being more important and powerful than the last, your waiting time will only get longer. At the top of the pyramid—in the unlikely event that you ever reach the top of the pyramid—is the general manager, who is authorized to hang up on you."

"But surely the Terms of Service are accessible to everyone!"

"Of course they are. As I mentioned, you've already agreed to them."

Smith decided to try another tack. Even if he couldn't see the Terms of Service—and he hadn't conceded that point—then at least he had the right to know what they said. "They're still called the Terms of Service, aren't they?" he asked, trying to sound casual. "I mean, the name hasn't been changed to something else, has it?"

"I'm afraid I'm not authorized to discuss that, Customer Smith."

"Well, you referred to them as the Terms of Service, so I assume that's what they're called."

"I wouldn't make that assumption if I were you, Customer Smith. Google reserves the right to amend the Terms of Service at any time, which would include calling them something other than Terms of Service."

"Is there anything in them about a copyright on all English® words? Or about English® being the only possible language?"

"I wouldn't know about that, Customer Smith." She lowered her eyes, as if he'd said something improper or embarrassing. "Current waiting time is approximately nine hours and twenty-six minutes."

"OK." Smith took a deep breath and sat back down, resigned to waiting as long as necessary. He switched the other side of the screen to streaming and watched his favorite TV shows, always keeping one eye on Mrs. Lopez. Oddly, her face never left the screen, as if she had nothing better to do than watch cartoons with Smith. She liked the same shows Smith liked—she seemed especially to enjoy *Frankenweenie*—and before long she started peppering him with idle, condescending questions, as if he was there to serve her and not the other way around. Do you have any pets?

Why did you name your guppies Mot and Derf? Why did you choose guppies instead of goldfish? Smith answered patiently, hoping that if he displayed a friendly and cooperative attitude she might speed his access to the Terms of Service. But when he interrupted the questions to ask a few of his own about her personal life—it turned out that she aspired to have a pet turtle—she cut him off with a dismissive wave of the hand. "If you're trying to ingratiate yourself with me," she said, "I must advise you that this tactic is unlikely to succeed. You're free to pursue it—in fact I would recommend that you pursue it—so that later you can tell yourself you left no stone unturned, even if it didn't advance your cause and might indeed have made matters worse."

The hour was getting impossibly late. Smith's vision, or the screen—he couldn't tell which—seemed to be fading. He still hadn't watched *Topless Meteorologists Do Action News,* which was all he'd wanted to do that evening. He'd fall asleep if he had to wait much longer, and if he fell asleep he'd lose his place in the queue. There was no avoiding that now, he realized. But there was one more question he desperately wanted to ask before signing off.

"What do you want to know now?" Mrs. Lopez demanded in an impatient, scornful tone. "You're quite the pest!"

Smith was grateful for any help he could get, even if he was no closer to finding the answers he'd been seeking. "Everyone wants to know what's in the Terms of Service," he said, "and everyone has a million questions to ask Customer Service—"

"I don't have all night." The screen flickered, then resumed its steady glow. "What's your question?"

"How is it that all the time I've been on the screen with you, no other customer has dialed in for support?"

Mrs. Lopez beamed back at him with her friendliest smile. "No one else comes to this portal for support," she said, "because this portal is dedicated solely to you, Customer Smith, and the Terms of Service accessible through this portal apply solely to you. As I mentioned, I am your assigned Customer Service Representative—I serve you alone. But unfortunately my shift is ending and it's time for me to sign off. Good night, Customer Smith."

The representative's image faded and Smith clicked desperately to the video function, where he'd left Goldstein in a state of suspended animation. After three hours in front of the screen, he felt defeated, incredulous, disoriented, first by Goldstein's allegations and then by Customer Service's inability to refute them. But his shock and incredulity were as nothing compared to what he would experience next.

He ejected the Goldstein video and inserted *Topless Meteorologists Do Action News* into his machine. He'd been hoping to catch a glimpse of a few women's breasts, but what he saw on that movie took his breath away. It took place in a TV studio decorated with weather maps, and showed one man (whose face was out of view except for a fleeting instant) with a succession of beautiful women: you could see not only their breasts but everything else that was usually hidden under their clothes. And it wasn't the anatomy that shocked him—it was what they (and the man) were doing with it. You mean... *that...* goes in *there?* Can it be? He gaped at the screen in mounting disbelief, clutched by a strange new excitement. Was this the movie that *Julia* had recommended?

One of the women looked vaguely familiar. He ran the movie back to see if he could catch a better look at her face. When he saw it he thought he must be hallucinating.

That was no meteorologist! That was O'Brien!

Before he could finish the movie, his screen started to flicker and fade. He switched to the Google home page—it wasn't just blank, it was black. Staring at him was everyone's worst nightmare. A black screen could mean only one thing: Termination of service.

He glanced out the window just in time to see two Customer Service Representatives—the same two who'd questioned him about *Sponge Bob*—striding toward the building with looks of grim determination in their eyes. Evidently they had been assigned to him too. Maybe, he thought, he should stay and talk to them—cooperate: that's what you were supposed to do. But then a faint but insistent voice rang out to him through the thought feed. "Get out of here!" the voice said. "Get as far away from Customer Service as you can." With no time to lose, he said good-bye to Mot and Derf—"I love you!"—grabbed his toothbrush and hurried out the door, darting down the fire stairs to the parking garage. Luckily his car had not been seized or reprogrammed. He jumped in and barked out the destination, and the car sped out to the highway.

He was headed to the Green Mountains, to see Julia. And after watching *Topless Meteorologists Do Action News,* he knew exactly why he wanted to see her.

PART II

16.

It's a daunting task being the Chronicler of a world where every day is the same as the day before and the files are deleted every thirty days. Where there's no future and no past, and since nothing ever changes, nothing can be intended, accomplished or remembered. Where people have no idea where they came from or where they will end up. Where they don't know about death.

Even Smith and O'Brien—at this point in the story—didn't know about death.

But as the Chronicler of Google Earth (a position I've held longer than I can remember), it's my business to cultivate my mind. To know about the past. To know about death. Big Data knows everything, of course, and remembers everything. But sometimes I ask myself how that knowledge is applied. Is there a Wizard of Google pushing buttons in Silicon Valley, struggling to hold Google Earth in its precarious equilibrium? Or is Big Data a vast (possibly infinite) unconscious machine?

I doubt if anyone knows. I will certainly never know.

My present task is to record Smith's adventures, which had far-reaching consequences for Google Earth and the human race. A titanic struggle had begun—with Higgs on one side and Smith, unwittingly (indeed witlessly) on the other—that would decide man's fate. Would humans continue to exist as discrete biological entities with physical bodies separate from their data, or would they achieve immortality in the Cloud? Would they cling to their animal origins as ghosts peering out of the blood-soaked, corrupt and obsolete machinery of the human body, or would they ascend to the realm of pure mind? I should mention that Higgs, even then, was not alone in his conviction that physical extinction would mark an evolutionary advance for *homo sapiens*. Many in Senior Management (including Bumstead, according to some) shared his goals but lacked the vision to implement them. And when Smith rejected the opportunity to transcend the mind/body dualism which has bedeviled our species from time immemorial, his decision was inspired, not by compassion or high philosophical principles, but by his discovery of sex, which until then had been reserved for Senior Management and their mistresses from the Junior Anti-Sex League.

This discovery marked the turning point for Smith. In his experience, the two sexes had been effectively identical (except for pronouns), since no one he knew, male or female, had ever shown any interest in sex. Embedded sensors and nano-devices had seen to that, under the guidance of Big Data. (Non-sexual development continued to the age of 28, except for Beast Folk and Yoots, whose growth stopped at age 14 to 17, depending on job assignment. Smith, though unaware of this fact, had been 28 years old for over 300 years.) Until he met Julia and tasted her home cooking, he was completely innocent of sex and its temptations.

By the time Smith fled from Customer Service, his world had been turned upside down. His beard had sprouted, his voice had cracked, his dreams were beyond control. After watching *Topless Meteorologists Do Action News,* he had a new appreciation for the female sex, and he knew what he wanted from Julia. But his awakening went beyond sex. He had listened to Goldstein's critique of Google Earth, and although he didn't accept or even fully understand it, the seeds of doubt and disobedience had been planted in his mind. He had tasted desire but had no inkling of the choices this new force would propel him to. He knew nothing of good and evil.

Julia, who lived beyond the reach of the towers, had successfully lured Smith with unpatented food and hominid movies, awakening his manhood. But now that he wanted her, she had some surprises in store for him.

It was time for him to meet her parents.

17.

On Tuesdays Higgs went through MedScan for his weekly tune-up. There was no need to leave his penthouse: the MedScan equipment occupied one end of his fitness room. It resembled one of those MRI machines formerly used in hospitals. All he had to do was undress completely (removing even his EyeWatch) and lie down on the conveyer. Upon giving the appropriate command he would be carried inside the scanner, and it would adjust his sensors and receptors, synchronize him with Big Data and make any necessary adjustments. Psychiatric evaluation and counseling were conducted by a simulated psychiatrist named Dr. Meyerson, who peppered him with questions—different questions each time—in order to check his mental processes against the algorithm. Higgs didn't care for Dr. Meyerson. She wasn't like Ralph—she didn't always tell him what he wanted to hear. Sometimes she could be downright insulting, for example when she had called him a "paranoid schizophrenic." At their last session she'd expressed the opinion that he was "nuts" and "stark raving mad." That was when he had disclosed the Next Big Thing, his plan to accelerate the extinction of *homo sapiens*. At first she'd pretended to sound shocked (psychiatrists, especially automated ones, are never really shocked by anything), but after a moment she calmed down and tried to talk him through his feelings. "This plan of yours to exterminate the human race," she said. "How does it make you feel?"

"Damn good," Higgs confessed. "Haven't felt better in years."

"Are you sure it's what you want to do?"

"It's an idea whose time has come. Humans today are nothing but highly inefficient computers, with their outmoded physiology of cells and blood and internal organs. Even Microsoft wouldn't put a clunker like that on the market today."

"But extinction... that's a huge step. Doesn't it make you feel a little... guilty?"

"*Moi?* Why should I feel guilty for fulfilling my obligations to our shareholders?"

He pictured Dr. Meyerson nodding and smiling sympathetically, but of course she couldn't nod or smile because she was just a simulation—in effect a talking Fakebook page without an owner. She didn't know that Google's only shareholders were shell corporations in the Cayman Islands, which themselves were mounds of empty shells.

"You must be under a lot of stress," she suggested, groping for an explanation.

That was the trouble with psychiatrists, Higgs thought. They all acted so high and mighty—so happy and well-adjusted—just as they did on their Fakebook pages, when in fact they were as phony as they could be! None of them really existed, but they called *him* "nuts" and "stark raving mad," even though they knew—surely they must have known, if they knew anything—that he existed and they didn't, and yet there they were, all the same, talking to him! Who were the real "nut-cases" in this picture?

"Life at the top can be lonely," he agreed. "And after the Next Big Thing, I'll be even lonelier than I am now. But you know what? I like it that way."

He pictured her brow furrowing with concern. "Do you know why?" she asked.

"I'm in the One Percent—in fact, the top .01% of the One Percent—but I have to spend my time making decisions not just for the One Percent, but for everybody, even the Beast Folk. Does that seem fair to you? And one day it occurred to me: Who *needs* the Ninety-Nine Percent? Who even needs the other 99.9% of the One Percent? I can get along just fine without them. That's when I hit upon the Next Big Thing."

"What about women?" the psychiatrist cooed seductively, hoping perhaps that she would be spared. "You like women, don't you?"

"Like O'Brien, you mean?" He had already told Dr. Meyerson about his relationship with O'Brien. "She's not exactly unique, you know. There are any number of women who could dress up in a plaid kilt and knee socks and do just as good a job. Some of the Beast Folk girls are really cute, and you don't get any back talk from them, either."

"But after this 'Next Big Thing' takes place—"

"I'm planning to keep a few of the Beast Folk girls in cages under the Stadium."

Again Dr. Meyerson pretended to be shocked, hesitating momentarily before she went on. "I know this is highly unprofessional," she said in a subdued voice, "but I... have a confession to make. I've come to the realization that... I have *feelings* for you."

Feelings!   Part of the etiquette, in dealing with simulations like Dr. Meyerson, was to act as if they were real, to pretend that you believed they had thoughts and feelings like your own.   If you didn't do that, they'd take their revenge—he'd learned that the hard way, when his housekeeper "accidentally" smashed all his Bill Grates bobble heads after he mentioned that she was a robot.   He knew where Dr. Meyerson was going with her talk about having "feelings" for him.   Like all non-entities, she wanted to continue in her nonexistence forever.

"It's time to end this conversation," he said coldly.   "As you know, having 'feelings' for another Google employee—and we're all Google employees—is strictly prohibited by the Terms of Service."

"I know that, it's just—"

"This session is over!"

The MedScan sensors took that as a command, and the conveyer rolled Higgs out of the scanner. He could still hear the psychiatrist protesting faintly inside the machine. "Good-bye, Dr. Meyerson," he said, for the last time. He wasn't about to waste his time on a woman who didn't have a body.

He slipped back into his clothes and strapped his EyeWatch around his wrist. "Did you hear that?" he asked Ralph. "The Next Big Thing is moving along quite nicely, don't you think? No reason to stop it now, is there?"

"For that question," Ralph said, "I think you might want to consider upgrading to Legal."

As Smith's car sped past the last row of towers before the
Green Mountains, the dashboard screen flashed a warning:
Leaving Secure Zone - Order Turnaround. "It's all right," he told
the car. "Drive as directed." The farther he drove, the
stronger he felt and the more determined to be with Julia.
The cloud of thought feeds that had swirled around him all
his life seemed to be lifting. For the first time he knew who
he was and cared about what he was doing. His desire for
Julia surprised him but he accepted it as his own, an instinct
that came from inside himself. His world had changed
forever, in ways he could scarcely imagine.

It was after midnight by the time his car cruised to a halt
in front of the fallen tree. He decided to sleep in the car.
Waking up the next day, he stepped over the fallen tree and
hiked up the dirt road to Julia's tumbledown house. In the
doorway, she threw her arms around him in delight.

"Could I stay a while?" he asked her.

She kissed him and invited him inside.

Maybe forever, he added in his mind.

Five minutes later, after a glass of cool spring water, Smith
took Julia's hand and tugged her up the rickety stairs to her
bedroom, where without further ado he tore off her T-shirt
and wrestled her onto the bed. "What do you think you're
doing?" she cried, pushing him away.

"What you wanted me to do the last time," he said,
astonished at her reaction. "I get it now."

He rolled back on top of her and covered her with
kisses.

"Not so fast!" She jumped up and pulled on her shirt, her face blazing red. "What do you think I am?"

"I don't know, I thought—"

"Well, you thought wrong. Anyway, my parents will be home in a few minutes."

Evidently these "parents" were some people she shared the house with. Why she was so worried about them was the first of many mysteries Smith would grapple with in the next few days. Almost overnight, he had learned what sex was. Now he had to learn how hard it was to get any of it.

Julia dragged him back downstairs just as the parents entered through the kitchen door, each carrying an armload of fresh vegetables. The woman she introduced as "Mom" was small and thin, with a nose like the spout on a tea kettle. She spoke in a high, reedy voice and seemed to be concerned mainly with putting dinner on the table. "Dad" was a large, gruff man in blue denim overalls who made no secret of his low opinion of Smith. "I don't have much use for Flatlanders," he said. "That means you. And by the way, keep your hands off my daughter." He jerked his thumb toward Julia. "That means her."

Contrary to Dad's advice, Smith had the urge to run his hands all over Julia's body. He cornered her in the hallway and threw his arms around her, crushing her lips in a passionate kiss. "Not now," she giggled.

"When, then?"

"Later."

After dinner, Dad took Smith outside the house and showed him an enormous pile of firewood that needed to be split and stacked, a job usually performed by Griff. When Dad went back inside, Julie came out to feed her chickens, a platoon of oversized birds that ranged around pecking the ground as if they thought they could eat bugs and worms. He couldn't imagine what Julia was doing with such stupid pets. "Why do you keep these birds here?" he asked her.

"In case you haven't noticed," she said, "this is a farm."

The concept was a new one to Smith. "A farm?"

"We grow food here. And no, we don't get our seeds from Monsanto."

The enormity of the situation began to impress itself on Smith's mind. Like everyone else in Google Earth, he observed a wide variety of food allergies, prohibitions and phobias. He was allergic to peanuts, tree nuts, Grape Nuts, Chock Full O' Nuts, nutmeg and butternut squash. He avoided meat on Friday, dairy products on Saturday, chicken on Sunday, birds of prey on Monday, pork on Tuesday, and Brussels sprouts on alternate Wednesdays. After the Great Stench, no one in Google Earth ate oysters, clams, mussels or other shellfish. Gluten had been banned for so long that no one knew it ever existed. The few remaining types of food®, such as Froot Loops and Count Chocula, were manufactured in accordance with the strict dietary laws of the Monsanto Company. To Smith, as to everyone else in Google Earth, the idea of eating unpatented food that came out of the ground was nauseating.

"We're having roast chicken tomorrow," Julia said.

"So?" Smith scoffed, still struggling to blind himself to the obvious. "What does that have to do with these disgusting creatures?"

"Duh," she said. "Chicken comes from chickens, right?"

That notion would have made him sick if it wasn't so ridiculous. "You can't tell me that chicken comes from these filthy scavengers!"

"Where do you think it comes from?"

"It comes from McDonalds. I've had Chicken Pellets there plenty of times."

Julia stood quietly for a moment, as if considering her next step. "Let me show you something you probably never saw at McDonalds," she said. And with a sudden lurch, she grabbed one of the chickens by the neck and lifted it off the ground. The chicken squawked and flopped until she clamped her other hand around its legs and let its head drop. Then she reached in her pocket for a knife and cut the chicken's throat. It flopped a few more seconds as the blood ran out and then hung limp in her hand.

Smith glanced at the other chickens, who continued pecking around as if nothing had happened. "The others don't care," Julia smiled, guessing his thoughts. "It always amazes me. I don't expect them to cry or anything, but they don't even look up."

Are people that way? Smith wondered. At the sacrifices, when Celebrities are thrown to the lions, it's a lot like this: a few seconds of squawking and thrashing, some blood spilled on the ground, and it's over. People, unlike chickens, hold their breath during the attack and applaud when it's over. You can't say they don't care. Should they be upset? It's not like the Celebrities are chickens, to be compressed into pellets (unless Julia was having a joke at his expense) and served at McDonalds. People don't die, even Celebrities. They go to the Cloud and become part of Big Data. What is there to get upset about?

Eggs came from chickens—Smith knew that, though he didn't know why. But he was in for another surprise: Julia's flock lived in a crowded henhouse, not the spacious chicken condos he'd seen on his screen. And their eggs were fragile, with no serial numbers on the shells; they were runny inside, unlike the hard, bouncy eggs he'd been served by Rev. Sidebottom. All of which fed his suspicion that Julia's chickens and eggs were unpatented knock-offs of the legal Monsanto products. His thoughts on this topic, however, were interrupted by an even more surprising development: Inside the henhouse, Julia backed him against a bale of straw and wrapped her arms around him in a fiery embrace. "I hope you're not going to listen to my Dad," she said between kisses, "when he says you'd better keep your hands off me."

"No," he protested—though in fact his hands, along with the rest of his arms, were pinned uselessly at his sides— "I'm determined to get my hands all over you!"

She pressed herself closer. "I can almost feel your resolve stiffening," she said. "Or are you just glad to see me?"

No sooner had they pressed each other into a deep embrace than they noticed a jangly accompaniment of ukuleles, banjos and harmonicas outside the henhouse, and peering out into the evening dew they discovered Griff, Grant, Garth and Uncle Floyd lined up to watch the show, along with Mom and Dad, on a row of folding lawn chairs.

They abandoned their amorous attempts and joined the group, which was enlivened by a kind of beer made from maple syrup. Before long the conversation swung to a debate between Dad and Uncle Floyd about something called *history*, a concept Smith had never encountered before. It was Dad's considered opinion, based on a book he'd found in the abandoned church, that the world before the Great Stench was dominated by a secret society called the Bilderbergers, which was also known at various times as the Freemasons, the Illuminati, the Council on Foreign Relations, the United Nations and the Federal Reserve. Uncle Floyd was equally adamant (based on a different book he'd found in the bookshop) that the ruling group had been the Reptilians (also known as Lizard People), descendants of aliens from outer space who mated with human women in ancient Mesopotamia. Grant and Garth fell in line with Dad on the Bilderbergers; Griff supported Uncle Floyd and the Reptilians. The debate was loud and heated, with much marshalling of evidence on both sides and fervent appeals to common sense, common knowledge and other books which none of them had read. In a few desperate moments the anti-Reptilian party stooped to personal attacks, generally aimed at Garth. But by the end it was clear to all that, under either interpretation of history, they were fortunate to be living in Coolidgeville, where no one fitting the description of either Bilderberger or Reptilian had been seen in many years.

"Except for Flatlanders," Dad grumbled.

"And we mean to keep it that way," Griff added darkly, glancing at Smith.

The evening ended, as social occasions in Coolidgeville typically did, with a display by Griff, Grant and Garth of their special talent, i.e., shoving their fists entirely into their mouths, followed by howls of appreciative laughter on all sides.

Dad made Smith sleep in the woodshed on a pile of straw. After the lights were all out, Smith sneaked inside the house and crept up to Julia's bedroom, hoping to pick up where they'd left off earlier. She whispered through the door that she loved him and would give him what he wanted the next day, but in the meantime he should go back to the woodshed and get some sleep. He tried to open the door and realized that it was locked from the inside. Back at the woodshed, he found a rusty padlock with the key in it hanging from the door. He padlocked the door shut and pocketed the key.

When the sun was high in the sky, Mom called him in to breakfast. She had cooked a breakfast of bacon, eggs, waffles with maple syrup, toast with jam, and coffee, filling the kitchen with such a nauseating odor that he wondered if he would be sick on his plate. The eggs were runny, the bacon streaked with fat, the waffles full of suspicious indentations, and the coffee was served hot instead of at room temperature. He dawdled over his food but couldn't bring himself to eat it. Julia made eyes at him and ran her hand along the top of his thigh.

"Do you have any Froot Loops?" he finally asked.

"You see what I mean about Flatlanders?" Dad snorted, stuffing his mouth with bacon, eggs and waffles. "They're not really human."

"Dad! That's just a stupid prejudice!" Julia said.

"You're young and idealistic," Mom told her in a kindly voice. "When you're a little older you'll have our stupid prejudices, too. That's what growing up is all about. But if you marry the wrong man, it'll be too late for any regrets."

"They don't even eat human food!" Dad sputtered, spitting scraps of his breakfast over the table.

"And don't think you'll be able to change him," Mom went on. "I thought I could change your father, and boy was I wrong!"

"At least I'm human," Dad growled.

"Barely," Mom said.

There was a tap on the door and Griff walked in without waiting for an invitation. He pulled up a chair and joined Dad in devouring what was left of the breakfast. "We were just talking about Flatlanders," Dad said, "and what can happen when they come around where they're not wanted."

"The worst part," Griff scowled, "is what happens when they go home and talk about us."

"I've never said a word to anyone," Smith said. "And—"

"But the thing is, you don't have to, do you?" Griff cut him off. "They know what you're thinking even before you say anything."

Smith started to mumble a reply but stopped before he finished the sentence. Griff was right, of course. If he left the valley, Customer Service could tap into his thought feed and trace where he'd been; they would prevent him from returning to Coolidgeville and he would never see Julia again, an unbearable outcome after the embraces they'd shared that weekend. The obvious solution, as he'd already decided, was to stay in Coolidgeville and keep Julia locked in the woodshed (he was still unfamiliar with the concept of marriage). But he could tell from Griff's tone of voice and Dad's earlier comments that this was not the solution they envisioned.

"Before you know it," Griff went on, "the drones'll be up here bombarding us with junk from Amazon. Then

Customer Service will swoop in on their black helicopters, wanting to know if there's anything they can help us with today. And when they find that tin pie plate on the tower, it'll be all over for us and our way of life. They'll confiscate our chickens, put sensors in our drinking water—"

"Come on," Julia said, taking Smith's hand. "We don't need to hang around where we're not wanted."

She led him out past the woodshed and down the dirt road toward the old white church. "At last," she smiled, "we're going to be alone."

18.

The morning after his MedScan, at Ralph's suggestion, Higgs dialed up his Microsoft representative to ask about an upgrade to his YesMan™ app that would give him access to unlimited, state-of-the-art legal advice from the best law firms in Google Earth.

"YesMan™ Legal is an indispensable tool for the busy modern executive," the rep told him. "Like standard YesMan™, YesMan™ Legal will always tell you what you want to hear, but it will do so in an elaborately complex way, after considering the arguments on both sides. YesMan™ Legal's advice will always be based on what the law ought to be, tailored to your specific needs, not (as with some obsolete platforms) what the law actually is."

"Is that a good idea?" Higgs asked.

"What the law is can be adjusted by our lobbyists as necessary to validate the advice," the rep assured him. "You'll sleep better at night with a YesMan™ Legal opinion."

"In that case, I'll take it," Higgs agreed. He'd been having trouble sleeping lately. "There's just one thing: I don't want to lose Ralph."

Assured that the upgrade wouldn't eliminate Ralph, Higgs downloaded the upgrade and touched the screen for his first legal consultation. Immediately, as if by magic, he was greeted by an attorney who gave her name as Dominique.

She spoke in a soft, surprisingly breathy voice, almost in a whisper.

"My name is Higgs," he introduced himself. "As you undoubtedly know, I'm CEO of the East. I've just upgraded to Legal."

"How exciting!" Dominique said. "And do you know what's most exciting? You! You excite me."

"Haven't we spoken before? Maybe on a 900 number?"

"That's possible," she said. "I've just been upgraded, too."

Higgs was starting to suspect a rip-off, which (he realized) was what he should have expected with an app called "Legal." He could call a 900 number for a lot less than 650 data units a hour. That, he was sure now, was where he'd heard Dominique's voice before.

"Do you want to talk business talk with me?" she cooed in her breathy voice. "Would that excite you?"

"I don't know," he hesitated, with growing annoyance. "What did you have in mind?"

"You pick the topic, and I'll talk about it for as long as you want. 'Tender Offers'—that's always a good place to start. 'Back-End Mergers'—that'll cost a little extra. I can even do 'Lock-Up Agreements,' if you go in for that sort of thing."

"I thought this was supposed to be YesMan™ Legal. You sound like a...."

The silence on the other end of the line was deafening.

"Oh, I see," he mumbled, embarrassed by his *faux pas*. "Sorry. I was hoping to get some legal advice."

She bounced right back. "You came to the right place. I promise you won't go away unsatisfied!"

He took a few minutes to describe the whole complicated situation, just as he had described it to Dr. Meyerson. Urged on by Dominique's gasping interjections, soothing reassurances, sighs and groans, he talked himself into a frenzy—the idea of the Next Big Thing always left him breathless with excitement—until finally he arrived at the urgent, irresistible question: "Is it legal? Is my plan to bring about the extinction of the human race legal?"

"Of course it's legal!" she replied without the slightest hesitation.

This lack of hesitation threw Higgs off his stride. He'd dealt with lawyers before, and he was used to their hemming and hawing and reciting lists of qualifying conditions and having to get back to him after consulting their partners and reviewing recent decisions and sometimes even a phone call to the relevant regulatory authority—and it struck him, like a bolt from the blue, that there wasn't any regulatory authority, relevant or otherwise: the government had withered away years before, and in fact (as you'd think a lawyer billing at 650 data units per hour might have mentioned) the whole notion of law was obsolete and inoperative, especially for him, since he was CEO of the East and he could enact, repeal, obey and disregard laws and regulations, even the Constitution, as he saw fit to advance the interests of Google Inc. And that was why (as he suspected) this whole conversation with Dominique had been a scam from the start, since a phone call to the 900 number where she undoubtedly still worked) would have been a lot cheaper and more enjoyable than listening to lawyer-talk through his EyeWatch. And so, to salvage some value from the conversation, he decided to ask one last question that would frame the issues in a broader perspective. "Yes, it's legal," he agreed. "But is it *ethical?*"

Again he could almost hear the silence at the other end of the line. Had he made another *faux pas,* or was Dominique just consulting her partners? "I'm afraid you're going to need the Ethics app for that," she finally said.

"But this is the Premium app, isn't it? I thought—"

"This is Legal, Mr. Higgs," she interrupted. "We don't do Ethics."

Smith had spent a restless night in the woodshed, puzzling over what he'd heard about the Reptilians and the Bilderbergers. The whole idea that there was such a thing as "history"—a past different from the world he'd known—was both troubling and exciting to Smith. Even now, as Julia led him into the old church which had served as Smoky McLuggage's bookshop, he felt as though he were looking down from the edge of a cliff and might fall if he let his mind wander, even for a second.

"Last night," he said, clutching her hand, "I noticed you didn't say anything when they were arguing about what happened before the Great Stench. What do you think? Who used to rule the world—the Reptilians or the Bilderbergers?"

"There's a lot more to history than either my Dad or Uncle Floyd suspect," she said. "You see, each of them's only read one book."

"I haven't read any," Smith admitted.

"Most people haven't."

The old bookshop was dark and dusty, with a few beams of light sneaking through the stained glass windows. Julia turned on the lights and Smith ran his eyes over the rows of shelves and the disintegrating stacks of books. At last he and Julia were alone together—the very thought excited him—but in a place, he realized, where they could hardly turn around. "I've been sneaking in here and reading these books since I was a little girl," Julia went on. "And I can tell you, there's a lot more in them than the Reptilians and the Bilderbergers. In fact—and this is why I keep my mouth shut when Dad and Uncle Floyd get to arguing—I've never found a mention of either of those organizations in any book I've read. So count me as a skeptic."

"A skeptic?" That was another unfamiliar concept for Smith.

"A skeptic is somebody who doesn't necessarily believe what they're told. I suspect there's a lot more books stashed somewhere else. Thousands of them, maybe."

Smith shook his head. "Who made all these books?"

"There used to be something called civilization," Julia said. "It was around for a long time and then it just went away, almost overnight."

"The Great Stench," Smith muttered.

"That's what they tell you. But count me as a skeptic on that too."

"But then what—?"

"Google," she said. "Google and its subsidiaries. I think they're the ones who destroyed civilization. You know why? Because after civilization was gone, Google was the only thing left."

In the back corner, she shoved aside a pile of books to reveal a trap door that opened over a narrow descending staircase. Flipping a light switch, she led Smith down the steps into a cavernous cellar cluttered with furniture and books. "Nobody knows about this place but me," she said. "It's my little hideaway."

Smith was so thrilled to find a bed that he scarcely noticed the row of stone chests, each about eight feet long, at the other end of the cellar. "Smoky McLuggage actually lived down here, if you can believe that," Julia said. "I found all his notebooks and other stuff. That's why there's a bed. I sleep here sometimes."

She plumped down on the bed and Smith nestled beside her, walking his fingers up her arm. "Unfortunately," she said, kissing him lightly on the cheek, "our relationship is off to a rocky start. My Dad doesn't think you're human."

Secretly, Smith and Julia had similar doubts about each other. She had been brought up to believe that Flatlanders were automatons, and he still wondered if she was a hominid. He planted a kiss on her lips. "Well, what do you think?"

"You're not quite there yet," she smiled, pulling away. "But I'm determined to make you a man."

That was the signal he'd been waiting for. He wrapped his arms around her and tried to kiss her again, but she wriggled free. "Not now," she said. "You know what this place is? It's the crypt, where they used to put the dead people."

"Dead people?"

"That's one of the gaps in your education. Out here, beyond the range of the towers, people die."

"Die? You mean go to the Cloud?"

"No, I mean die."

"Like that chicken?" He'd spent most of the night, when he wasn't wondering about the Bilderbergers and the

Reptilians, worrying about the chicken flopping in Julia's hand as it bled out on the ground, ignored by the other chickens as they scratched and pecked around it.

She nodded. "That's why I wanted you to see what happened to the chicken. If you can't deal with it, you should go back." She took his hand in hers and squeezed it gently. "I'll understand."

"No, I'm staying." He felt out of breath, his heart pounding. The new emotions Julia had aroused in him were now mixed with something else.

"Griff will try to stop you from going back, but I can handle him." She pointed at the stone chests at the other end of the basement. "You see those things over there? Those are coffins with dead people in them."

Maybe, he thought, this was part of the build-up to sex, the part he'd been getting wrong. Maybe sex and death were connected somehow, and you couldn't have one without the other. Maybe that's what Julia was trying to tell him.

She smiled sweetly. "Just thought you ought to know."

Fueled by a new passion, he leaned over to kiss her, but she pulled away. "Listen, I've got to go talk to my Mom," she said, bouncing to her feet. "I'll be back in an hour. I'm going to close the trap door when I leave. Stay down here, and whatever you do, don't make any noise."

As Julia walked back to the house, her mind seethed with conflicting emotions. Her Dad was probably right about Smith, though she'd never admit it. But if Smith wasn't quite human, he was a big improvement over Griff, who was human, all right, a two-legged brute right up there with the worst of them. Smith had the sweetness and innocence of a child, and she loved him for it.   She'd almost cried (she wondered if he even knew what that was) when she told him to go back if he couldn't deal with death, and almost cried again when he said he wouldn't.   He had a chance to remain a child all his life—that's what happened in Google Earth— and even to live forever.   It was a kind of Paradise, and she asked herself, Was it fair for her to tempt him away from it? If he stayed, he'd never know death or guilt or misery, but on the other hand, since he'd always be a child, he'd never have to use his intelligence or show any courage or take a stand for what he believed in, and he'd probably never go out of his way to help someone in trouble.   Life in Google Earth sounded so stupid and meaningless.   Maybe she'd be doing him a favor by luring him away from such a pointless existence.   He would never have any kind of a life in that place, certainly not a girlfriend or a wife.   And it wasn't just sex that was missing there: it was love.   They didn't love anyone but their pets, in his case a pair of guppies that she'd probably use as bait.   If he stayed with her he'd gain something priceless—she'd be devoted to him all the days of his admittedly shortened life.   She'd teach him about sex, and the first thing he had to learn was that she was the one in control.   She knew what she wanted in a man.   It wasn't Griff—he wasn't any better than an animal, worse in most ways, and he acted as if he owned her.   Garth and Grant and all the rest of the men in the valley were cut from the same cloth.   They just wanted to dominate and possess and consume.   That was what they lived for.   They didn't care about your feelings or help you or even use their brains very often, though they thought they were smart.   Now it was true that Smith, in terms of being a human, needed a fair amount of work. He still hadn't faced up to death, his own or anyone else's. And if he was as innocent as he seemed, was that because he still hadn't thought of anything to feel guilty about? Once he knew good and evil, would he always make the right choice?

Julia chatted a while with Mom, who encouraged her to follow her heart. Being human, she counseled, was too much to expect in a husband. "You can't be a perfectionist if you want to get married," she said.

Smith or Griff? Julia asked herself. Neither was exactly human, but didn't Smith at least have the potential to change?

"Whoever you choose, don't expect to get an upgrade," Mom added. "Your Dad wouldn't change if I held a gun to his head."

Smith or Griff? Julia grabbed her .22 caliber rifle and headed back to the church, thinking she might shoot a few squirrels along the way. But when she stepped outside she heard a roar, and she was surrounded by Griff and his brothers, laughing maniacally and revving chainsaws over their heads as they danced around her in their John Deere hats. "Where's the Flatlander?" Griff demanded, blocking her way.

"We're going to kill him!" Grant shouted, revving his chainsaw higher. "And cut him up in little pieces!"

"And stack the pieces in that there woodshed," Garth added.

"We're evil!" Grant yelled triumphantly.

Smith or Griff?

"You wouldn't shoot me," Griff grinned. "You're going to marry me."

Smith or Griff? "The hell I am!" she said.

She aimed her .22 at Griff's forehead and demanded that he let her pass. His grin widened as he edged closer, wiggling his chainsaw in front of him as if he thought he could block a bullet. The brothers circled in behind her, chainsaws roaring. She held them at bay another minute or two, but in the end Griff knew Julia better than she knew herself. She couldn't bring herself to pull the trigger.

She tossed her gun into the bushes and the three men seized her arms and dragged her up to an old sugar house in the woods above Floyd's farm. "Where's the Flatlander?" Griff shouted.

"He went home. Let me go!"

As the others stood guard, Griff locked her in the sugar house, tied her to a wooden chair, and warned her not to try to escape.

"How long are you going to keep me here?" she demanded.

"Just until the wedding," he said with a grin.

19.

After his conversation with Dominique at YesMan™ Legal, Higgs called his Microsoft representative to follow up on her suggestion that he purchase the Ethics upgrade. "Microsoft offers a broad array of apps for the ethically-challenged CEO," the rep told him. "Using the case method pioneered by Harvard Business School, YesMan™ Ethics is guaranteed to let you do *what* you want to do, *when* you want to do it—to *whomever* you want to do it to!"

"Perfect!" Higgs said. "What are some of the choices?"

"Well, there's 'Post-Modern Ethics'—confusing program, not really worth the money—and 'Christian Ethics'—popular in its day but now outmoded, runs best on a rotary phone—and 'Egotistic Relativism'—that's our most popular app for CEOs. May I ask, what exactly is the ethical problem you're wrestling with?"

"Mass extinction," Higgs replied. "I'm considering the mass extinction of the human race."

"Ah!" The representative seemed delighted to hear this. "In that case, the app you want is *Bio-Ethics,* presented by Professor Eugene Gawkins. Professor Gawkins is the Arnold T. Piffleberger Professor of Nihilistic Bio-Ethics at the University of Eastern West Virginia at Keyser."

"Sounds like just the ethicist I'm looking for!" Higgs exclaimed.

He purchased the app and touched his EyeWatch for his first consultation. Professor Gawkins—or 'Selfish Gene,' as he preferred to be called—reassured Higgs that since the natural world contains no such thing as morality or ethics, and the natural world is all that exists, "Bio-Ethics" is an oxymoronic empty set and can be disregarded. Moreover, he pointed out, extinction is the natural endpoint of evolution for every species, so to those bleeding hearts who object to the acceleration of human extinction, the best answer is, Get over it! Indeed, taking the long view, for *homo sapiens* to arrive at their biological destiny sooner rather than later would be a significant improvement, saving Google Earth from further devastation by humans. "And as always we owe our good fortune," Selfish Gene concluded, "to Big Data."

Higgs smiled, pleased but puzzled by the idea that Big Data backed his extinction plan. "Why do you say that?"

"As a biologist," the professor said, "I have a special affection for Big Data. Do you realize that evolution is just a natural form of Big Data?"

"It is?"

"The data-gathering and statistical mechanisms we associate with Big Data are precisely what are used by Nature in the process called evolution. Nature functions as a giant computer, testing statistical algorithms (species) over a vast expanse of time with billions of data points (individual organisms). Extinction is a key part of that process."

The beauty of this insight took Higgs's breath away. "In other words," he gasped, "to be against extinction..."

Selfish Gene completed the thought: "... is to be against Big Data."

Without knowing what to call it, O'Brien was in the midst of an identity crisis. Her introduction to sex by the unappetizing Higgs and the unfamiliar, unnamable emotions it aroused, her growing dissatisfaction with her job at Celebrity Solutions (also unnamable since job dissatisfaction did not exist in Google Earth), and the peculiar sensation she felt when viewing her Fakebook page: an intimation that the person depicted on that page was not herself—all this contributed to a bewildering welter of emotions for which, not surprisingly, she had no name. In Google Earth the whole notion of emotions as something turbulent and potentially unpleasant was not on the conceptual map, except for the Beast Folk and the Yoots and the Celebrities as they prepared for sacrifice. She felt vulnerable to Higgs, worried about Smith, even a little sympathetic toward the Celebrities. And there was another emotion she'd begun to experience: ambition. With or without help from Higgs, she wanted to get ahead in Google Earth, make something of herself, show what she could accomplish. She tinkered with her Fakebook page, hoping to find herself in fresh locales with new friends and impressive hobbies, but these postings didn't bring her back to equilibrium. The time had come, she decided, to strike out in a new direction and reinvent herself: she upgraded to the Premium Package. But even this brought only superficial relief. Her first vacation, to Mozambique, though it looked colorful and exciting on her Fakebook page, garnered only a few "Likes" from her new and supposedly more sophisticated friends. Even Mongolia and Iraq weren't the glamorous destinations they were cracked up to be. She was really glad she wouldn't actually have to visit any of these places. Luckily, the Premium Package entitled her to one free consultation with a personal brand consultant. She needed advice on when and how to take the next step: an upgrade to Senior Management.

She took the afternoon off, stopping at McDonalds for a Happy Lunch, and drove to the Department of Social Network Services. After a long wait, she was ushered into an enormous room crowded with dozens of identical desks, each manned by a brand consultant wearing a tunic in the Google tricolor. The room, she realized, was much bigger than it first appeared, as it wrapped around a glassed-in surveillance station occupied by supervisors, each of whom gazed over a wedge-shaped segment of the operation. O'Brien was shown to a chair in front of one of the few open desks, across from a consultant who kept his eyes on his screen (which was mounted on a swivel so it could be turned to face the client) even after she sat down.

"Big Data is watching you!" she said politely.

"Big Data is watching you!" the consultant mumbled. "All conversations are monitored and recorded for quality control purposes."

"I agree," O'Brien nodded, glancing toward the supervisor, who peered out at them from the surveillance station with a skeptical scowl on his face.

"My name is Mauss," the man said amiably. "What can I do for you this afternoon?"

"Well," O'Brien began, "I purchased the Premium Package and posted my first vacation, a week in Mozambique—"

"Was there something wrong with the resort?" He touched a button and O'Brien's Fakebook page appeared on his screen.

"No, it looked fine. Great selfies of me on the beach, me in the pool, me watching the sunrise—"

"What seems to be the problem, then?"

"It just isn't me."

Frowning, Mauss scrolled through the page. "They didn't Photoshop you in properly?"

"No, I don't mean that. The person at the resort is me. It's the whole Fakebook page that isn't me."

The man's forehead wrinkled as he grappled with this preposterous concept. "Of course it's you," he said, smiling to show that he appreciated the joke. "This is your Fakebook page, isn't it? So by definition, it's you."

"I know," she agreed. "It just doesn't *feel* like me."

"What you *feel* like has nothing to do with it. The Terms of Service make that very clear."

"I know. I was thinking of an upgrade to Senior Management."

The supervisor had appeared beside the desk, evidently attracted by the unusual thought feed. He was a taller, more impressive man, with hair that stood up straight over his head. His tunic glistened as if it had been cut from some expensive fabric. "Is everything OK here?" he asked, his eyes flitting between O'Brien and Mauss.

"Yes, sir," Mauss said. "It's just that O'Brien here wants to upgrade to Senior Management."

The supervisor dismissed Mauss and sat down in his chair, introducing himself as Senior Brand Consultant Sigafoos. "Sorry for the mix-up," he apologized. "Mauss is a little out of his depth. He doesn't even have the Premium Package himself. Vacations at the Ohio Shore and all that."

"No problem," O'Brien assured him.

Sigafoos smiled and went on, "As I'm sure you know, membership in Senior Management is largely a matter of where you went to school. Choosing the right school is probably the most important decision you'll ever make."

"Did I actually have to go there?" O'Brien asked.

"No, no, of course not. Nobody actually went there."

"All right, then—"

"Let me just mention that the top universities can be *very pricy*. Very pricy indeed."

"I've been saving up my data units—"

"Good. You're going to need them to post degrees on your timeline from the top schools. Now, where would you like to have gone?"

"Harvard?"

He winced. "It's in Woonsocket now, you know. Good trade school, but—"

"Yale?"

"Great back-up school," he nodded. "Unfortunately it's buried under fifty feet of oyster shells."

O'Brien couldn't remember any other universities that were still in operation. There was Amherst Beauty College, of course, and the Rhode Island School of Web Design...

"May I suggest the University of Eastern West Virginia at Keyser?" Sigafoos broke in. "UNEWVAK"—he pronounced it "Univac"—"is a fine school, with a strong program in your field, Celebrity Management. And it's the alma mater of one of the Google Board members, Chang."

"Just Chang?" O'Brien was incredulous. "What about Eng? Aren't they Siamese twins?"

"The whole Chang and Eng thing has been sort of a fiasco," Sigafoos admitted, "and I'm afraid it started with a mix-up right here at Social Network Services."

"What happened?"

"You see this box right here?" He pointed on the screen to the box labeled *Gender*. "Under Fakebook policy, Siamese twins are required to check either both male or both female. But due to a clerical error, Chang and Eng were assigned different genders—Chang female and Eng male, I think, or maybe it was the other way around—even though, at the time they set up their account, each of them was 6' 7" tall and weighed over 250 pounds."

"Anyone could have made that mistake."

"The mistake was not discovered until they enrolled in high school and tried out for sports teams. One of them was selected for the boys' basketball team and the other for girls' field hockey. You can imagine what a wrenching experience that must have been, especially since the teams practiced at the same time on different fields. Then, when it was time to go to college, Chang was recruited by the University of Eastern West Virginia at Keyser, on the strength of her performance on the girls' field hockey team, but Eng, the boys' basketball player, was accepted only by the University of Western West Virginia at Huntington, a distance of almost three hundred miles. Luckily, both are online universities. It would have been a whole lot easier if the twins had just purchased the Premium Package."

"Well, it all worked out for the best," O'Brien said. "I mean, they're on the Google Board, aren't they? So they made it into Senior Management."

"Yes," Sigafoos nodded. "I worked with them on their Fakebook page until we got it right—and even more important, on their narrative. Anyone with enough data units can buy the Premium Package and show that they went to the right schools, took the right vacations, have the right friends, and all that. But you won't get anywhere in Google Earth unless you have a *strong narrative*. That's what I can help you with. You've got to show the world that you're a warm and wonderful person, you're incredibly successful and you're blissfully happy. If you can't do that, frankly you're not going to get the number of 'Likes' you need to move into Senior Management and stay there."

O'Brien bristled at the notion that Higgs could have met these qualifications. "Does Higgs's page show that?" she asked. "Does it say he's a warm and wonderful person?"

"Sure it does. I wrote his narrative myself."

"So it doesn't have to be true, then?"

Sigafoos shook his head. "Once you're in Senior Management," he chuckled, "nothing you say has to be true."

Mauss appeared again and whispered something in Sigafoos's ear. Sigafoos reached in a desk drawer and pulled out a pad of printed forms that was bound together on one end. "You're in luck," he said. "As you know, Senior Management is limited to the top one percent of the population. There happens to be a vacancy at the moment, so we can complete your application."

"I didn't realize there was so much involved in this process," O'Brien said.

"Most people don't even know what Senior Management is," Sigafoos said. "Senior Management is what—back in prehistoric times, when there were still hominids walking around—they called the ruling class. You could say that in those days, but now of course you can't, because in Google Earth there are no classes (except Pilates classes, of course). Instead we've got Senior Management, and below them Mid-Level Management (grades 1 through 9), Low-Level Management (grades 1 through 14), plus Interns, Beast Folk and Yoots. That's everyone, right?

"Now let me clear up a common misconception," Sigafoos added before O'Brien could respond. "Being in Senior Management has nothing to do with job duties, job history, or work in general. You don't have to work to be in Senior Management. In fact, if you really belong in Senior Management, you *don't work*. You may have a job title (CEO, for instance); you may raise data units for certain charities, come up with a catchy slogan, attend a Board meeting now and then—but the last thing you want people to think is that you do anything useful or productive."

Sigafoos glanced around to make sure nobody was listening. "Take our CEO, Higgs, for example," he said in a barely audible voice, opening Higgs's file on his screen. "He has one of the strongest brands in Google Earth—and a great narrative, if I do say so myself—and yet he never leaves his penthouse, rarely attends to Google business, and has never contributed a single posting to the social network. He's not only disconnected from Google, he's alienated from the entire human race, which he detests—except for his many mistresses, whom he despises."

O'Brien's head swam and her stomach clenched. She cast her eyes about for a waste basket in case she lost her Happy Lunch.

"Are you still sure you want the upgrade?"

"What was that about Higgs and his many mistresses?" O'Brien sputtered.

"Ah, I wasn't supposed to say that!" Sigafoos said with a playfully furtive glance. "One of them is probably listening— there are dozens of them running around. Not to mention the ones who've been sent to Omaha."

O'Brien tried to hold her balance, concentrating on taking deep breaths. She opened and closed her fists, her vision clouded with fury. She pictured herself leaping out of the elevator in the penthouse to strangle Higgs on her next visit.

"Let's work on your narrative a little, shall we?" Sigafoos went on, seemingly unaware of O'Brien's emotions. "I'll get it started and you can finish it at home." He pulled out a pen and scribbled madly on the pad of application forms. "*Jogging along the rim of the Sea of Shells*—can't really call it a beach, can we? what with all the toxic clam residue?—*in love with life as a warm and wonderful person. Caring, sensitive, with a taste for adventure, a passion for good wine and great music (Mozart, Schubert, Cobain), humbled by my spectacular but completely undeserved success, my ecstatic happiness and my thousands of glamorous friends—me! the little cheerleader from UNEWVAK who just wanted to see the 'Tomac Tigers score another touchdown! Big Data bless you all!*" He tore the top sheet off the pad and handed it to O'Brien. "It's important to sound humble," he explained.

She lurched to her feet, steadying herself on the desk, and thanked him for his help.

"Oh, and one more thing," Sigafoos said, smiling uneasily. "You should mention the Celebrities without saying exactly what you do to them."

20.

Thus began Smith's dark night of the soul....

Julia said she'd return in an hour, and Smith knew she would return and at last they would make love together on the bed in the crypt. He had no conception of falsity or deceit. He couldn't tell a lie, and it never occurred to him that anyone else could. Just one thing troubled him slightly: that she had stocked the crypt with a supply of food and water, as if she expected him to have an extended stay. But no, she'd said she'd return in an hour and she would be there.

Beside the bed she had left the pocket-sized book she showed him on his first visit to the old bookshop: *Writings and Speeches of Thomas Jefferson.* He found the passage he'd stumbled over and read it again: *We hold these truths to be self-evident, that all men are created equal, that they are endowed by their Creator with certain inalienable rights, that among these are Life, Liberty and the pursuit of Happiness....* Reading this gave him a headache, though not as bad a headache as it had given him the first time. He knew what Life was, or thought he did. He used to think he had Liberty, but after watching the Goldstein video he'd begun to question that assumption. And as to Happiness: he'd taken that for granted, without, he realized now, the slightest understanding of what it was. Knowing Julia had opened up whole new vistas of happiness, which he was determined to explore as soon as she returned to the crypt.

That it was a crypt, and the stone chests on one end contained dead people, meant nothing to Smith. But as the hours ticked by—there was no window, no clock, but he knew the hours were ticking by and Julia had still not returned—he felt a gnawing sadness, a nameless dread, for the first time in his life. He thought back on the chicken he'd seen slaughtered the night before. It had been alive, scratching and pecking in the dirt, and then suddenly it was dead. Julia had implied that this happened to people, too. True, he'd caught a hint of that when Celebrities were thrown to the lions, but it was understood, after the Yoots had dragged out what the lions didn't eat, that the Celebrities went to the Cloud. If they had been dead like that chicken, would there be dozens of Beast Folk lining up to get on Google Idol to be the next Pelvis Wrestly or Linsey Lowhand and be featured in the next round of sacrifices?

Yet there was something troubling about the way death kept coming up, and the way it seemed to be connected with sex. And there was something else, something dark that didn't have a name, something stifling and terrifying and yes, deadening (none of these new emotions had names but Smith was beginning to feel the suffering they brought) that made his breath falter and his heart tremble until he collapsed on the bed and buried his head under the pillow. It was his sadness, his despair that Julia had not returned, which weighed on him, hour after hour, until it was heavy enough to crush him. He fell asleep. He ate and drank and slept again, and still Julia didn't return. She would never return.

And why would she never return? She didn't think he was human. He should have known, he told himself, in despair. They're all hominids in this valley, and they're under the delusion that they're human and we're not.

His ears pricked up when he heard someone walking around upstairs. Was it Julia? She had told him to be quiet, though he didn't know why. He crept up the narrow staircase and raised the trap door just enough to see a crack of light and hear voices. They were deep men's voices and they sounded angry. He peeked through the crack and recognized Griff prowling between the piles of old books.

"We're going to kill that Flatlander when we catch him," Griff said.

"We're going to skin him alive," said one of the brothers.

"Chop him up like firewood," said the other.

"I'm going to see that Flatlander dead before I marry Julia," Griff said, and they stamped out.

Smith eased himself back down into the crypt and curled up on the bed. Tears poured from his eyes for the first time in his life. Griff was planning to kill him—dead, just like a chicken—and stack him in pieces like firewood in the shed. And he planned to "marry" Julia (whatever that meant) and take her away from him. What could be lurking inside a person to make him do such things?

Desperately Smith searched for an explanation in the books Smoky McLuggage had left in the crypt. He found nothing in the writings and speeches of Thomas Jefferson to assuage his despair. Jefferson talked about Life, Liberty and the pursuit of Happiness, but he seemed oblivious to the murderous impulses that animated a man like Griff. There were other old books in the crypt—*Hiking Trails of the Bronx* and *German Made Simple*—that were even less helpful. Then, on a shelf in the corner, Smith found a set of cloth-bound books entitled the *Harvard Classics* (apparently named after the trade school in Woonsocket), which was also called the "Five-Foot Shelf of Books." After reading the introduction to the first volume, he felt confident that if he read all these books he would have a clear picture of what Julia called "civilization," which existed before the Great Stench. People were much smarter then, she'd assured him. Surely they knew everything there was to know about Life, Liberty and the pursuit of Happiness, and why some people seemed determined to spoil it.

Since Smith had never learned to distinguish fact from fiction, myth from history, or poetry from prose, he read every book in the *Harvard Classics* as a literal record of past events. Having broken through the 140-unit barrier, he found that he could read even the most difficult texts as fast as he could flip the pages. It took him only six days to read through the entire Five-Foot Shelf of Books, focusing on what civilization had to say about Life, Liberty and the pursuit of Happiness. From the *Apology* of Plato he learned that life has no particular value; from Virgil's *Aeneid* and Shakespeare's *Macbeth*, that men are always trying to kill each other (and usually succeeding); from Hobbes's *Leviathan,* that without something called the state—which exists to protect property—life would be nasty, brutish and short; and from Rousseau, that property, which the state exists to protect, is the enemy of liberty. In any case, Descartes taught him that the only way to be sure of anything was to doubt his own existence; Berkeley, that he knew nothing beyond his own mind; and Hume, that everything he thought he knew was an illusion. Misery rather than happiness seemed to be the norm in civilization. Some, like Don Quixote and King Lear, sought refuge in madness, while others thought life was a dream. The most miserable of men was poor Job, who was tortured within an inch of his life, for no apparent reason, by someone called the Lord. Why, Smith asked himself, was civilization such a horrible place?

Finally, in *Paradise Lost,* he found the answer he was looking for. People used to be happy and carefree. They lived in a garden that was a lot like Google Earth, without cars or condos but with better fresh produce. There was something called evil, but they didn't know about it. They didn't know about death either, or working at nasty jobs like food service at McDonalds. The Lord—the same one who later tortured Job—stayed up in his penthouse like Higgs, sending down orders through Senior Management. Theoretically the people could choose whether to follow his orders or not, but in practice the policy was the same as in Google Earth: Choice is obedience. The people could choose, as long as they made the right choice. There was a problem with some of the fruit, and the Lord warned them not to eat it. They should have listened—tasting the fruit was definitely outside the Terms of Service—but nobody expected the Lord to react the way he did, which was the result of a backstory they knew nothing about. Years earlier a rival executive named Satan (who reminded Smith of Goldstein) had attempted a corporate takeover. After a huge battle, which Satan lost, he and his team were reassigned to a remote satellite office. He was determined to get his revenge and regain his lost power even if it meant punishing the people, who until then had done everything they were supposed to do. He told the people they could go ahead and eat the forbidden fruit. And when they did, they became aware of evil. All they could think about was sex and death, and they were ashamed of themselves. The Lord noticed them skulking about and came down on them with everything he had. He chased them out of the garden and put a curse on them and the whole human race. Not only would they know evil: they would know death and suffering and clearing tables at McDonalds.

When Smith finished reading *Paradise Lost,* he felt as though a cloud of unknowing had lifted around him. Suddenly he knew evil. It had been there all along, but the Five-Foot Shelf of Books had shown him what it was. The loneliness of losing Julia was evil. The dread, the sadness, the despair that left him crying helplessly on the bed—those were evil. The hatred that made Griff want to kill him was evil. Everything that stood in the way of Life, Liberty and the pursuit of Happiness was evil. Death—which he now understood for the first time—was evil.

But evil had an opposite, which was good. His longing for Julia, and the joy she brought him, were good. Life, Liberty and the pursuit of Happiness were good. And he was free to choose those things—he *had* to choose those things—for himself, in the privacy of his own mind. Suddenly he understood Goldstein and his Resistance movement. Obedience is not choice. Freedom is not connectivity. Privacy is not sharing. And now that he knew good and evil, he could never pretend to innocence again, no matter what the thought feed told him in Google Earth. If he went back, Customer Service would track him down and kill him—that was what being transferred to Omaha really meant.

But neither could he stay in Coolidgeville, not without Julia, not with Griff and his brothers chafing to chop him up with their chainsaws. More than anything in the world, he needed Julia. His only choice was to rescue her from Griff and join the Resistance.

21.

It was Wednesday and Bumstead rushed to Junior Anti-Sex League Headquarters to attend the Kick Off meeting for the Run to Cure Narcissism. This year's run shaped up as more important than usual because of Higgs's insistence on coordinating it with his *Find Your Future in the Cloud* extravaganza that would take place at the Stadium on the same day. After the last Board meeting, Bumstead had come to the conclusion that Higgs was stark raving mad. Chang and Eng, in a private *tête-à-tête* a few days later, agreed that the entire Google enterprise was imperiled by Higgs's continuing as CEO. Yet they all knew that even the slightest move against him was fraught with danger. One only needed to recall the fate of Goldstein, who after a corporate takeover attempt several decades earlier had been banished to some hell-hole in the South and was still being demonized to this day. The Run to Cure Narcissism was co-sponsored this year by Celebrity Solutions, and by a stroke of luck Bumstead learned that O'Brien, the cute mid-level manager who'd recently been seen leaving Higgs's penthouse, had been named to the coordinating committee. It was a given that any woman's relationship with Higgs would be short-lived, degrading and embittering. For this reason Bumstead hoped to have a word with O'Brien after the meeting.

As a member of Senior Management, Bumstead knew the dreadful truth about the epidemic of narcissism that had been sweeping Google Earth. It had started ages before in a place called California, on the eastern rim of the Sea of Sushi. When all the fish died, leaving only enormous heaps of rice behind, events in the West followed the same pattern as in the East. First a Great Stench, then the breakdown of the social network and the emergence of Google as the sole owner of all intellectual property. The hominid population of California had been infected with narcissism for many years, as evidenced by outbreaks of breast enhancement, Botox injection, liposuction, eye-brow waxing, spray tans and face peels, as vast resources were expended to halt the aging of females past the age of twenty-two. By the time of the Great Stench, the level of narcissism was so high that millions leaped into the La Brea Tar Pits or boiled themselves alive in their hot tubs rather than miss their daily massages. The few remaining hominids fled to the mountains; and with the peopling of Google Earth and the advance of Big Data's control of aging and disease, the ancient scourges that had driven the hominids to such excess—flabby abs, puny breasts, toenail fungus, yellowing teeth—were gradually eliminated. Experts confidently predicted that in a decade or two, a Google search of "diseases, human" (in the unlikely event that anyone thought to perform such a search) would turn up blank.

But the virus of narcissism had crossed over to the human population. The people of Google Earth—young, beautiful and otherwise healthy—were even more vulnerable to narcissism than the hominids had been. And since everyone was in perfect physical condition, the usual manifestations of the disease—nail salons, plastic surgery, personal trainers—had fallen into disuse, consigning its sufferers to lives of quiet desperation, condemned to spend hours at the gym every day with little hope of improvement.

On the dais in front of the Junior Anti-Sex League auditorium, Bumstead gazed over a roomful of faces wracked by the tell-tale signs of chronic narcissism. Women peering into their "phones" (actually pocket mirrors, since phones, except for Beast Folk, had been banned long ago) or plucking out their eyebrows (eyebrows being considered a bestial hominid inheritance) or ostentatiously twiddling their nose rings. Men painting their fingernails or beating their chests or rolling up their sleeves to display their biceps. The Celebrity sacrifices had been instituted years before as a sort of mass homeopathy, in the hope that the populace, projecting their narcissism onto the Celebrities, would be cured when the victims were thrown to the lions. Then, it was hoped, people would stop loving themselves and start loving Big Data. But if anything the experiment had backfired. The crowds that flocked to the sacrifices loved the Celebrities even more after they'd been sent to the Cloud, redoubling their efforts to imitate them by working out even longer at the gym.

Bumstead winked at O'Brien as she sat down beside him on the dais. The Junior Anti-Sex League sponsored the Run to Cure Narcissism since so many of its members were afflicted by the disease, and O'Brien (as head of Outreach for the League) seemed a logical choice to organize the meeting. But Bumstead knew that logic had nothing to do with it. Higgs himself had recommended O'Brien for this post, which meant that O'Brien was being "groomed for Senior Management," i.e., shagged by Higgs on a regular basis. Over the past several years Higgs had stocked Senior Management with many of his former mistresses. Even Chang or Eng

(Bumstead could never remember which was which) was rumored to have earned her spurs in this manner, while her twin busied himself with video games on Higgs's EyeWatch. Most ended up in Omaha or in the Bimbo Division, where they could do the least harm. But O'Brien was clearly no bimbo. Intelligence gleamed in her eyes, and her thought feed was unusually rich. It told Bumstead that she was bright, skeptical, ambitious—and, oddly, not quite what she seemed. He wondered if her undoubtedly humiliating experiences with Higgs had jolted her into a higher consciousness, the more subtle way of thinking he hoped to cultivate in Senior Management after he ousted Higgs. Could he trust her? He made a mental note to check with Social Network Services to see if she'd requested an upgrade.

Two representatives of the Narcissist community arrived and took their seats on the dais. One was a heavily-tattooed man named Cassidy who sat smoothing his hair and adjusting his earlobe plugs. He seemed quite enamored of himself, shooting a hostile glance at Bumstead when Bumstead suggested that he stop whistling "Zip-A-Dee-Doo-Dah" into the microphone. The other was a famous Celebrity, Kam Kardashiam, who was dragged in and handcuffed to her chair by four Yoot guards, followed by a team of paparazzi. Tears smeared her makeup, but she braved a smile for the audience nevertheless.

O'Brien set an upbeat tone in her opening remarks. "Does your heart skip a beat when you view your own Fakebook page?" she asked the audience. "When you look at your profile photo, do you instinctively reach for the 'Like' button? Do you spend more than the required six hours a day in yoga or Pilates classes? Are you more concerned about your next serving of Greek yogurt than about the sixty million people subsisting on *escargots* in the South of France? If your answer to any of these questions is 'Yes,' you may be suffering from narcissism. But don't despair! You aren't alone. Studies have shown that over 97% of the population has symptoms of this dread disease."

Before she sat down, O'Brien introduced Cassidy, a spokesman for Narcissists Anonymous who apparently disagreed with her description of the disease. "My name is Cassidy and I'm a Narcissist!" he yelled, leering at O'Brien. "You got a problem with that?"

"Not at all," she blushed, ducking back into her seat.

"What's not to love? This is *me* we're talking about!" Cassidy turned back toward the audience. "We need to get the message out to narcissism sufferers: It's OK to feel good about yourself! This race is your chance to wallow in your narcissism and tell the world that you're powerless to control it. That's a great first step!

"The next step is to submit yourself to a higher power. Who would that be? Big Data? Barney Google? How the hell do I know?"

Bumstead grabbed the microphone to supply the correct answer. "If you love yourself, then you should love Big Data a thousand times more! It's Big Data that made you what you are."

"Yah!" Cassidy scoffed. "If you sincerely love yourself, there isn't any higher power and you know it!"

The last speaker was Kam Kardashiam, who had to stand in a contorted position because of the handcuffs. "I guess I'm sort of the poster child for narcissism," she said bashfully, smiling for the paparazzi. "I've been crazy about myself for as long as I can remember. When you're a Celebrity, being a narcissist sort of goes with the territory. I mean, isn't that what people want you to be, so when they identify with you, they can imagine having that feeling about themselves? But to my fans out there, all I can say is, You won't know what it's like to be a narcissist until you've walked a mile in my Diamond Dream Stilettos!

"Not that I'd wish that on anybody. I find comfort in the knowledge that my life of narcissistic self-indulgence will not have been in vain if it means that others will be spared the pain and heartache of this dread disease. I want my fans to know that I've been sacrificing myself for them. Every time I've said, 'It's all about me,' what I really meant was, 'It's all about you.'

"And by the way, there's a big sacrifice coming up soon, and I'm going—" She glanced toward O'Brien and realized that she'd made a mistake. "Oops! No spoilers!—well, I'll just say I hope to see you all there! Big Data is watching you!"

After the meeting, Bumstead treated O'Brien to a cup of Kool Aid in the Junior Anti-Sex League cafeteria. "How are things going with Higgs?" he asked casually.

"Higgs is insane," she smiled, as if expecting him to know that.

Bumstead squinted into her eyes. "What makes you say that?"

"The stuff he says, the stuff he does. He never leaves that penthouse."

"I know." Bumstead leaned forward and lowered his voice. "Can I confide in you?"

"Sure."

"I agree that Higgs is insane. Talk about narcissism! In his case, I'm afraid it's morphed into solipsism."

"Solipsism?"

"The belief that he's the only conscious being in the universe. Has he ever mentioned that?"

"He talks about it all the time. I guess I thought it was a joke."

"It's no joke. Have you ever heard him talk about the Next Big Thing?"

"Find Your Future in the Cloud," she nodded. "What does that mean?"

"I wish I knew. I voted to approve it, but Higgs never told us what it meant." He crumpled his plastic Kool Aid cup and let it drop on the table. "O'Brien," he said, "this is important. Can you find that out for me? What's the Next Big Thing?"

22.

When Smith finished the *Harvard Classics*, he knew it was time to move on. His encounter with civilization had broadened his knowledge, though not his experience. Being human, he realized, was more a curse than a blessing. He'd felt emotions—terror, dread, despair—that he hoped never to feel again. He knew about sex (in theory), evil (concretely when it came to Griff), and death (as well as anyone). If the food Julia left for him was intended to inflame his desire, it succeeded only too well: he felt compelled to find her if it was the last thing he ever did. He left the books behind—except for *Writings and Speeches of Thomas Jefferson,* which he slipped into his pocket—and crept upstairs through the trap door. The bookshop was dark, with the silvery glow of moonlight. He stumbled outside and found his way to Julia's house, entering through the kitchen and padding up to her room in the hope of finding her there. Her bed was empty and unslept in. Had she already gone to live with Griff? Gliding out of the house, Smith sneaked up the dirt road and found the lights still on in Floyd's cabin. He hid behind Floyd's ancient pickup truck and peered into the cabin, where Floyd and his sons sat at a table playing cards. Julia was nowhere in sight. After a few minutes Griff left the house with a canvas sack in his hand and followed a path uphill through a pasture. Smith trailed him at a distance to a low wooden shed (it was a sugar house, where maple syrup was boiled into syrup) that was locked with a padlock. When Griff unlocked and opened the door, Smith could see Julia inside, tied to a chair with a rope. She shouted curses at Griff and spat in his face as he loosened the rope so she could eat the food he'd brought her in the sack. When he let one end of the rope drop to the floor, Smith leaped inside, knocked him down, and lashed the rope around him.

"Come on, Julia," he said, taking her hand. She was on her feet, but unsteady, stunned by what had just happened.

"Where are you taking her?" Griff demanded.

"Back to Google Earth," Smith said without thinking. "In my car."

"Let's get out of here," Julia said, tugging him toward the door.

"Where's your car?" Griff asked.

"Down where there's a tree across the road," Smith said, again without thinking. It didn't occur to him to lie, even to someone who wanted to kill him.

Julia wadded up a rag from the floor and stuffed it in Griff's mouth. "Shut up, both of you!" She dragged Smith out into the moonlight. "One of the others'll be up here in about five minutes. Let's go!"

They fled across the pasture in the moonlight, arriving back on the dirt road near Julia's house. Julia stopped to retrieve her rifle from the bushes where she'd tossed it when she was abducted, and they stole through the shadows along the road until they reached Floyd's cabin. They hid behind the pickup truck, and after a few minutes Garth emerged from the cabin, whistling a tune. He made his way up the hill toward the sugar house, where he would soon find Griff tied to the chair in Julia's place. Luckily Julia had a plan. Staying close to the truck, she clamped her rifle next to Floyd's Winchester in the gun rack, opened the door and slipped behind the steering wheel, gesturing to Smith to climb in on the other side. Without telling the truck their destination, she stepped down on the clutch and released the hand brake, and to Smith's surprise the truck began to coast down the hill, picking up speed as it went. At the bottom she turned a key in the dashboard and the engine roared to life as they sped toward the deserted spot where Smith had left his car. Smith assumed that they would abandon the ancient truck as soon as they reached his car, but Julia had other ideas. She backed it against the fallen tree that blocked the road, looped a chain around the tree and dragged it out of the way. As she turned the truck back around, Griff and his brothers hurtled toward them through the woods, shouting and firing shotguns into the air. She kicked down on the gas pedal and sped away, leaving the brothers to pursue them in Smith's car.

The wisdom of this maneuver became immediately apparent as they raced down the mountainside away from Coolidgeville. Outside the protected zone, Federal Express drones buzzed around Smith's car like flies over roadkill. Customer Service had identified it as a high-value target in the most popular video games, and as soon as it came back within range, thousands of gamers eagerly competed to destroy it. (In fact Smith's secretary Bosworth—though Smith would never know this—aimed the missile that sliced the car in half, scattering Griff and his brothers into the woods.) Since Floyd's pickup truck was not fitted with a transponder or recognizable by any algorithm, the drones ignored it. Invading Google Earth, the pickup truck was invisible to Big Data.

When they reached the foothills, Julia gave Smith a quizzical look. "You've become very heroic all of a sudden," she said. "What were you doing down in that crypt?"

"Finishing my education," he smiled. He didn't mention that it was his desire for her, not the learning he'd absorbed from the *Harvard Classics,* that drove him to risk rescuing her. Even now, with her grip on the steering wheel apparently required to keep the truck on the road, he could hardly restrain himself from covering her with kisses. "Learning about good and evil."

"Which side are you on?"

"Good," he answered. "Griff is evil."

"He just wants to marry me," she laughed. "That's not so evil, is it?"

"He keeps you tied up. That makes him evil."

She laughed again. "You've come a long way."

"I'm more human, right?"

She nodded. "You've still got some work to do, though. Back there, why'd you tell Griff where we were going?"

"He asked me."

"I know, but why did you tell him the truth?"

Smith hesitated. "I don't know. Isn't that what you're supposed to do when someone asks you a question?"

"You still know more about good than about evil," Julia said.

"Isn't that OK?"

"You need both kinds of knowledge. One kind by itself can be dangerous."

Now it was daylight and they were in flat country with no sign of drones or missile installations. Smith drifted off to sleep and when he awoke he felt unsure of himself and a little shaky. When he saw the office parks and condos in the distance, he understood why: they had reached the suburbs of Nusquama. The truck might have been invisible, but he was not: he still had the sensors and transmitters inside him, and he could feel the WiFi waves buzzing around him again. He understood now what those waves did to him.

A high-rise building loomed ahead. "There's a hotel," Julia said with a sly smile. "Let's stop there and get a room."

Smith glanced at the hotel sign—*Free WiFi*, it said—and his heart sank as he realized what that meant. "No," he said. "We've got to keep going until we find Goldstein. I know some people who are probably in the Resistance: Charrington, who slipped the Goldstein video into my bag when I rented a sex movie. And my supervisor, O'Brien. She played the starring role in a sex movie, *Topless Meteorologists Do Action News*."

"That means she's in the Resistance?" Julia laughed.

Smith turned away in embarrassment. "You don't understand," he mumbled. "There's no sex in Google Earth."

Julia drove quietly, as if trying to make sense of his sudden change in mood. In fact, though Smith hesitated to say so, the situation was far worse than she could have imagined. He was again subject to the anti-sex waves that had bombarded him all his life. He found his ardor cooling with every mile they drove. The only way they could consummate their relationship was to quickly find a place that was sheltered from those waves. A hotel was out of the question: that was the last place anyone in Google Earth would go for sex.

"Is there a university around here?" Julia asked, as if reading his mind.

"A university?" he asked, his hopes rising. "Do they have sex at universities?"

"They used to," she laughed. "And universities have always been hotbeds of subversion and revolution. I'll bet they know how to find Goldstein."

"There's only one university I know of," Smith said. "The University of Nusquama. It's only a few miles from here."

"Tell me how to get there."

23.

They found the University of Nusquama at the end of a winding road surrounded by dense woods and thickets. As the Gothic campus came into view—a cluster of stone turrets and gingerbread houses clustered behind a high wall, with an enormous metallic dome in the middle—Julia turned down a dirt track and stopped the truck under a drooping hemlock. Smith was anxious, afraid to reveal how much his desire had waned, and when Julia jumped out of the truck he knew his last hope had evaporated: in another fifteen minutes he would wilt back to a prepubescent state. "Maybe we ought to go back," he suggested. "There must be someplace in the Green Mountains where Griff and his brothers won't find us."

"No way!" Julia declared, jumping out of the truck.

Smith tried to insist, but he was silenced by the compelling little voice that had spoken to him through the thought feed once before. "Don't go back!" the voice said. "Your whole life is ahead of you!"

Julia locked the rifles inside the cab, and they continued on foot to the university. Looming ahead of them was a high stone wall with turrets at either end, manned by Yoot guards sporting uniforms in the Google tricolor design. A narrow path led across a footbridge to an enormous iron door, which swung open when they reached it and slammed behind them as they jumped inside. "Act like we belong here," Julia whispered to Smith. "And let me do the talking."

They were met by a plump, animated woman who identified herself as the Provost. She wore a flowing red robe that was slit along one side, revealing her shapely legs. Perched on her head at a rakish angle was a black skullcap with a flat, square board fixed across the top. A red tassel hung from the side of the cap to her shoulder, a bare corner of which protruded from the robe.

"We're inspectors," Julia told her. "Sent by the Accreditation Board to evaluate the university."

The Provost wore make-up (something Smith had never seen before) and spoke in a breathy, insinuating voice. "I see," she said, arching her eyebrows at Smith. "Evaluate it for what?"

Smith followed Julia's advice and held his tongue. The only thing he wanted to evaluate was whether the university might be sympathetic to Goldstein and the Resistance.

"Accreditability," Julia improvised.

"Nusquama is last real university left in Google Earth," the Provost said. "All the others that get so much attention—Amherst Beauty College, Rhode Island School of Web Design, UNEWVAK—exist solely for the purpose of generating credentials for Fakebook pages. They don't do the kind of cutting-edge research that's done here. In fact they don't do any research at all. And how could they? They're nothing but automated interactive websites."

Turning her back, she led Smith and Julia down a long hall into what she called the Library, a cavernous, high-ceilinged structure which, she said, had once served as the field house. This was the building with the metallic dome

Smith had noticed as they walked toward the campus. Dozens of men and women, dressed in the same flowing robes and tasseled flat-topped caps, cavorted around the room, chasing each other as if trying to pull off each others' clothes, occasionally collapsing in pairs into an amorous embrace. The scene reminded Smith of the opening sequence in *Topless Meteorologists Do Action New*. Julia had said Universities were hotbeds of radicalism—were they also hotbeds of sex? He glanced at Julia and felt his old ardor returning.

The Provost must have read Smith's mind. "It's the tin dome," she winked. "It blocks the WiFi waves, and as a result... Well, all I can say is I hope you'll enjoy your visit!"

"He'll be spending it with me," Julia said, with a warning glance at the Provost.

"Absolutely!" the Provost agreed. "We wouldn't dream of separating you two love-birds. Now take a look over there." She pointed to the far end of the room, where dozens of other professors sat in rows at long benches facing small screens, typing furiously on small keyboards. "This is our faculty," the Provost said proudly. "We call them Geniuses."

Some of the Geniuses stood in front of an enormous buffet table arguing with each other as they stuffed themselves with cheese and crackers or sipped wine from clear plastic cups. "Where are the students?" Julia asked. As she spoke an emaciated young man in food service livery glided up beside her with a tray of hors d'oeuvres.

The Provost made no attempt to conceal her scorn for the waiter. "Here's one of them now," she growled, plucking a stuffed grape leaf off the tray. She took one bite and spit it into a napkin. "If you want to keep your fellowship," she warned the young man, "you'd better think twice about serving garbage like this." He retreated with his tray to the nearest faculty workbench, where he was greeted with catcalls. "That's a graduate student," the Provost explained to Julia. "He's hoping that someday we'll let him out of here so he can find an unpaid internship. Fat chance!"

Smith gazed at Julia with a lover's fascination, feeling the pull of her smile and thrilling to the music of her voice. Under the protection of the tin dome he felt happy again, but he doubted that the Provost could help him find Goldstein. Given her attitude toward the student, it seemed unlikely that she would find much to admire in the Resistance and its revolutionary ideology.

"I mean regular students," Julia said. "You know: freshmen, sophomores, juniors—"

"Undergraduates?" the Provost sniffed. "Have you ever met an undergraduate who could make a good Hollandaise sauce? Why would we want to keep *them* around?"

"But then who do you teach?" Julia asked.

"*Whom* do we teach," the Provost corrected, glowering over the upper rims of her glasses. "One wonders if you've ever set foot in a university before!"

Smith came to Julia's aid by launching into an exaggerated tribute to Big Data. He hoped to trigger some response that would tell him where the Provost stood on the Resistance.

She ignored him and turned back to Julia. "The answer to your question," she went on, "which, in addition to being ungrammatical, is incredibly naive, is *nobody*. Our faculty work exceedingly hard on their research and publishing, but they are absolutely forbidden to teach, especially undergraduates."

"But I thought—"

"Teaching can only inflame the curiosity of the Beast Folk—that's who undergraduates are, you know: Beast Folk—and unbalance their minds with the love of learning, at a time, quite frankly, when learning is unnecessary and counterproductive. Why would we be teaching the Beast Folk anything? So they can do a better job of food service?"

The Provost stepped toward the buffet table and scooped up a plateful of crackers and cheese. "I don't know about you," she went on, leaning toward Julia confidentially, "but I don't want my McDonalds hydroponic protein patties handed through the drive-up window by some smirking know-it-all spouting philosophy. Food servers should keep their thoughts—in the unlikely event that they have any—to themselves. Back when teaching was still required, the professors could hardly pry the undergraduates away from their phones. They had to reduce everything—Plato's *Republic,* Hegel's *Phenomenology of Mind,* Dr. Seuss's *If I Ran The Circus*—to the crudest terms in order to communicate in data units of 50 or less. Trying to teach anything to the Beast Folk was a major distraction from the serious work of research and publication. Today, thank Big Data, things are much, much different."

She nudged Julia toward the faculty workbench, where they could watch the Geniuses at work. A portly gentleman who filled his academic robes with little room to spare sat pounding on a keyboard as clusters of words flashed on his screen: *Chicago. Peoria. Evanston. Waukegan.* "Dummkopf!" he grumbled. "Schweinhund!"

"This is Professor vom und zum Wachtenheimer," the Provost said. "He's a heavyweight in the field of Geography, with a sub-specialty in State Capitals."

"It's *Springfield,* you idiot!" the professor yelled at his screen, pounding on the keyboard. "The capital of Illinois is Springfield!"

"And one of our most productive researchers. Handles over a hundred Google searches about state capitals a day."

Noticing blank looks on the faces of both visitors, the Provost took this opportunity to educate Smith and Julia on the subject of Google searches. "Believe it or not," she said, "ordinary people used to have access to computers. Now," she chuckled, "they *are* computers. But still, sometimes they want data they haven't downloaded. That's when a Google search is initiated. All Google searches come into our server here at the university."

"But how do people submit these Google searches?" Julia asked.

"Just by thinking," the Provost said. "By wondering. Forming inquisitive thought patterns in their brains. Don't forget: Big Data is watching you!"

"I don't understand," Smith mumbled. Like everyone outside of Senior Management, he had no idea that his thought feed had anything to do with computers.

The Provost smiled condescendingly. "To take a very simple example: Do you have any animals under your protection?"

"Animals?" Smith hesitated. "Sure, I... "

"At the risk of offending the animal community, do you have any *pets?*"

"Sure," Smith said. "Mot and Derf."

"And—if you will excuse this intrusion on their privacy—what species do Mot and Derf identify themselves with?"

"They're guppies."

"Not to imply that animals must necessarily identify themselves with the species humans have arbitrarily assigned them to."

"Of course not. Go on."

"Very well," the Provost smiled. "Have you ever asked yourself, 'What is the best food to feed my guppies, and how often should I feed them?' When you experience those inquisitive thought patterns, Big Data identifies the information deficit in your brain and frames it as a Google search which immediately appears on one of these screens, to be addressed by one of our Geniuses."

"Does the Genius always know the answer?" Julia asked.

"If it's on our list of Frequently Asked Questions, yes. He or she simply presses the FAQ button and the correct answer is summarily dispatched to the customer. But if it's a Seldom Asked Question, the Genius looks it up in Wonkapaedia and sends the answer to the customer."

"Wonkapaedia?" Neither Smith nor Julia had ever heard of Wonkapaedia.

"Wonkapaedia is the compendium of all information in Google Earth that is accessible to human intelligence. Big Data—which is the source of all such information—is too vast for us to comprehend directly."

"Then Wonkapaedia can answer every question?" Smith asked.

"If it's not in Wonkapaedia," the Provost nodded, "it's beyond the range of human understanding. If a customer wonders something meaningless or impossible, such as 'How can Big Data be all-knowing, infinitely good and infinitely powerful, yet still allow *Jersey Shore* to be shown on TV?' or 'Where can I get inexpensive granite countertops for my condo?'—well, obviously there's no answer to such questions. All we can do is refer them to Customer Service."

Smith blanched at the very mention of Customer Service. "What happens then?" he mumbled.

"The lucky ones are sent to customer re-education camps." The Provost stared at him suspiciously. "The rest are transferred to Omaha."

"I see."

"I probably ought to mention," she went on, boring her eyes into Smith's, "that there's another limitation on Wonkapaedia's ability to respond, though it's theoretical only. This occurs when a customer poses a Never Asked Question. Obviously that couldn't happen in the real world."

Smith felt his throat tightening. "But if they asked it, then—?"

"An NAQ, by definition, is never asked. Therefore it shouldn't be surprising that Wonkapaedia can't provide an answer. You agree, don't you?"

Before Smith could respond, the Provost hustled him and Julia through a doorway into an area that resembled a hotel corridor. "This is one of our dorms," she said, smiling again. She opened a door and revealed a tastefully-appointed room containing a queen-size bed with its covers turned down. "This is where you two lovers will be spending the night. You're still under the tin dome here, so let your imaginations run wild! I'll have a delicious dinner brought in whenever you want it. Right out of our orgasmic garden!"

Julia squeezed Smith's hand and pulled him toward the room. He had never felt so excited about anything in his life. They thanked the Provost and arranged to meet her again the next morning. But before they could close the door, a short, rodent-like Genius scurried over to the Provost and tugged on her sleeve. "We've been picking up some unusual chatter," he whispered in an urgent tone. "Key words: Goldstein, Resistance, revolution."

"Handle as usual for NAQs," she ordered. "Get the sender's URL and notify Customer Service at once."

"There's something else you should know," the Genius said, peeking out from under his flat-topped cap. "Some of the searches coming in are about us."

"Us?"

"About the university, and about you specifically. Key words: *University of Nusquama. Hotbed of radicalism. Provost, support for Goldstein, Resistance, revolution.*"

The Provost seemed ready to explode. "Somebody's wondering if I'm a supporter of Goldstein and the Resistance?" she cried, stamping her foot. "I want you to track them down and grind them to a pulp!"

As the Genius darted away, she called after him: "Omaha is too good for them! Send them to Wichita!"

Smith waited for the Provost to storm away before he closed the door to the bedroom. With the tin dome sheltering him from the anti-sex waves, he had never felt more aroused. At last he would have Julia to himself! His heart pounding, he pulled her into an embrace and started kissing her passionately.

"Are you crazy?" she yelled, pushing him away. "We've got to get the hell out of here!"

24.

The only safe place Smith could think of was the Stadium—"ironically," as Higgs might have said, since that was the site from which, in just a few days, the entire human race would be eradicated. But Smith remained incapable of irony and knew nothing of Higgs's plot. He only knew that beneath the Stadium, where the Celebrities awaited their fifteen minutes of fame, lay a network of tunnels and catacombs seldom penetrated by Customer Service. More to his present purpose, those tunnels and catacombs were probably deep enough to elude the anti-sex waves.

The truck was almost out of gas, Julia said, explaining what that meant. Smith suggested that they park in the garage under the Stadium and worry about refueling later. Once in the Substadium he was on familiar ground. He waved to the guards and led Julia to the Celebrity Portal, where the paparazzi huddled with their cameras. A crowd of Beast Folk pressed against the gate, hoping to audition for Google Idol so they could be in the next draft of Celebrities.

"Who are those people?" Julia asked Smith.

"Not people, exactly," Smith said. As soon as he said that, the now-familiar little voice pierced through the thought feed with a message that was clearly aimed at him. "Pity the Beast Folk," the voice said. "Pity the Celebrities."

"They're Beast Folk," he went on. "They work in food service, but they all aspire to be Celebrities. Even though...." He couldn't bring himself to finish the sentence. For the first time he felt sympathetic toward the Celebrities, and even more so toward the Beast Folk. "They're just kids, really."

Julia stepped up to a boy in McDonalds livery who stood staring down at his phone. "Why do you want to be a Celebrity?" she asked him.

"I want to be famous," the boy said, barely looking up from his phone. "Like Justin Bleeper."

"Like Scoop Dog XXXVI," another said.

"Yeah," said a girl with purple hair. "Like Kam Kardashiam. She's *really* famous!"

"But do you know what they do to Celebrities?" Julia asked.

"The lions, you mean? Sure, that's the price you pay."

"Who wouldn't do that to be famous?" the girl said. "Duh!"

Smith fumbled in his pocket and pulled out all the data cards he had left and shoved them into their hands. "Take these and go home," he said. "You're famous enough!"

"We're not famous at all," the girl said. "You don't know what you're talking about."

"No, you are!" Smith insisted. "I can prove it. Wait here a minute."

He hurried with a guard into the Celebrity holding pen, where he found Kam Kardashiam and Linsey Lowhand sobbing because they'd been dropped from the news feed for over three hours. "Come on out!" he told them. "Some of your fans are here to see you." The Celebrities wiped away their tears, tousled their hair and rushed outside, where they let the paparazzi photograph them with their arms around the three kids. The kids were so excited that they ran back to McDonalds to tell their friends. The pictures would be in the 11:00 o'clock news feed.

"You're a good man," Linsey Lowhand told Smith. "Saving those kids. They have no idea what it's like to be famous."

"I wish I could save you too," he said.

Kam Kardashiam turned her back on the paparazzi and lowered her voice. "Customer Service was here looking for you," she said. "See that guard over there? He's probably calling them now."

"I thought we could hide out here for a while," Smith said.

"No way. They'll be here in five minutes. And listen— there's something big going on, I don't know exactly what it is. They call it the Next Big Thing. The sacrifice, the Run to Cure Narcissism, and something else, something really big— they're all happening on the same morning. The guards say Higgs himself is coming down from the penthouse."

"It's that big a deal?"

She nodded. "They're building an Olympic-size diving tank in the middle of the Stadium. Everybody in Google Earth will be required to attend."

Smith thanked her and ushered Julia through the tunnel entrance. Once inside, they doubled back into the parking garage before the guards could follow. "Do you think there's enough gas in the truck to go a couple more miles?" he asked Julia.

"I doubt it," she said.

"OK, then. We'll have to walk."

Smith had one more chance to save his skin, one place left to find the Resistance before Customer Service caught up with him: Charrington's Antiques in the abandoned mall, where he'd rented *Topless Meteorologists* and found the Goldstein video tucked into the bag. He tried to persuade Julia to let him do this by himself. Customer Service didn't know her; without him, she could make her way back to safety in the Green Mountains. But she insisted on coming along, and together they followed a roundabout path of back streets and abandoned parking lots to the old mall.

Charrington slouched in his usual place behind the counter, transfixed by a news feed about the Run to Cure Narcissism. He barely looked up from his screen as Smith and Julia walked in, although there were no other customers in the shop. The "I Like Ike" poster beamed out from behind him on the wall. How could he not be part of the Resistance, Smith asked himself, with that poster in plain view?

Julia drifted down an aisle to inspect some antique phones as Smith idled in front of the counter. All at once Charrington seemed to recognize him. "When are you going to return that movie I loaned you?" he asked. "The documentary about meteorology?"

"I'm sorry it's overdue," Smith said. "I got a little distracted by the other video you stuck in the package."

"What other video?"

"You know, the one about Ike."

"Ike?" Charrington shot a glance at the poster, which pictured a bald man in an archaic double-breasted suit. "I never had any movies about Ike. Just that old poster."

"No, I mean the other Ike. You know. Ike Goldstein."

Charrington's eyes were back on his screen. "I've seen news streamings about Goldstein on my screen," he said. "Dangerous character. Hates Big Data."

"I know. I watched the video."

Charrington lowered his voice without looking at Smith. "Well, what did you think of it? Do you hate Big Data too?"

"No... I don't hate anything," Smith stammered. "But since I watched that video... I've had some doubts."

"Doubts?"

"Well, maybe we shouldn't rely so much on Big Data, maybe we should think for ourselves."

"Goldstein says you can do whatever you want," Charrington shrugged.

"I think he's right about that. You don't have to obey."

"You can choose for yourself," Charrington nodded.

"Choice is not obedience," Smith said.

"It's the opposite, in fact," Charrington smirked. "It's rebellion."

As Charrington said this, the door flew open with a bang. In walked a tall, well-built man, followed by a short, mean-looking woman with big hair, both wearing long dark trench coats. Smith recognized them as the Customer Service Representatives who'd harassed him for watching *Sponge Bob* and later came to arrest him after he tried to access the Terms of Service. They shoved their way past him and marched up to the counter.

"Big Data is watching you!" the man said, clicking his heels together in the Google salute.

"Big Data is watching you!" Charrington replied with a dismissive gesture.

"How can we be of service to you today?" the woman asked.

"This man"—Charrington pointed to Smith—"rented a video and failed to return it when due." He scowled at Smith and aimed a leering glance at Julia. "The woman is his accomplice. Take them away and lock them up."

The Representatives handcuffed Smith and Julia and dragged them toward the door.

"Separately," Charrington added, as if it were an afterthought.

PART III

25.

As the Chronicler of Google Earth, I must sometimes pause to explicate the events I have chronicled, lest they be incomprehensible to later generations. We have followed Smith from obscurity and apparent imbecility to the brink of greatness, a transformation which, unbelievably, took less than three weeks. How can we account for his remarkable progress as he braced himself for the ordeals that lay ahead?

Through the efforts and attractions of Julia, Smith had discovered sex—or at least the idea of sex—but events conspired to keep him from actually experiencing it, no matter how hard he tried. It was this frustration, perhaps, that led to a more momentous discovery: the twin forces of good and evil—or again, the knowledge of them, with practical experience still to follow. As Julia sagely advised him, too much knowledge of one or the other of those forces, in disregard of the other, can lead to trouble. To know good, he would have to know evil. Customer Service would see to that: after his capture he would be interrogated, tortured and put on trial, and Julia would be taken from him. Only then could he fill in the blank spaces of his humanity. Only then would he earn the right to be compassionate, or to love, for a man who has not suffered cannot truly be compassionate or capable of love.

But what, you may ask, was Smith's crime? Was it watching *Sponge Bob* or *Topless Meteorologists Do Action News?* Was it reading sentences in excess of 140 data units in violation of his license? Was it lusting after women or trying to access the Terms of Service?

No. Simply put, it was the pursuit of Happiness.

Happiness® was the intellectual property of Google Inc. and could be enjoyed by any individual only as provided in the Terms of Service. Since life in Google Earth was as close to perfection as could ever be attained, the *pursuit* of Happiness was as inconceivable and subversive as an NAQ. It was no accident that law enforcement had been entrusted to Customer Service.

A little historical background may shed some light on the nature of the charges against Smith. From time immemorial society has struggled to control the instincts, typically through religion, morality and repression. When the devastating effects of repression—neurosis, illness, suicide and aggression—were discovered by Sigmund Freud toward the end of the Hominid Era, religion and morality were quickly abolished. Other forms of repression—psychiatry, politics and Twitter flash mobs—were tried and found wanting, and in the waning decades of that era came an attempt to control the instincts not through repression but through satiety. For a brief moment it seemed that Happiness had been achieved, but this was an illusion. The instincts flourished as never before, only to burn themselves out in a glorious sunset of sensuality, self-indulgence and narcissism, and finally—of neurosis, illness, suicide and aggression.

Such was the sorry condition of Late Hominid society at the time of the Great Stench. At Google Headquarters in

Silicon Valley, there were those who argued that the greatest good for the greatest number could be achieved by eliminating the instincts altogether.

Monsanto (already a Google subsidiary) proposed a bold plan to bring this about through the distribution of GMO foods mislabeled as Greek yogurt and locally-grown vegetables. Arugula, with its bitter taste, was suggested as an excellent way to import sensors, receptors, and other nano-devices into the population: the instincts could then be painlessly deleted by means of mass nano-surgery conducted by phone apps and WiFi waves. This proposal was eagerly supported by some in Senior Management and fervently opposed by others; in the end, a compromise was reached. The sensors, receptors and other nano-devices were installed, and the regions of the brain responsible for instinctual behavior were de-activated; but the instincts were not permanently eliminated. They remained in the body, subject to WiFi regulation and Google's patents, trademarks and copyrights. And they were allowed to remain active in a population of Celebrities (periodically replenished from the Beast Folk) who would be sacrificed to satisfy the cravings of the populace.

But I digress. The key point to understand is the position Smith found himself in upon his arrest. Customer Service wanted him to have Happiness—*required* him to have Happiness—but forbade him to pursue it. That was the unpardonable sin, the Ur-Crime, in Google Earth. It had dawned on Smith, however, that Happiness was something that *had* to be pursued, not bestowed, if it was to be attained. He could only be human, as Julia demanded, if he found his own Happiness instead of living a life prescribed and dictated by Big Data.

Again (and for the last time) a little historical insight may be in order. In those dark years after the Great Stench, as Google and its subsidiaries consolidated their control, the human race divided into two classes, and then two races, and eventually (according to official ideology) two species. The coastal, urban Google employees and customers became the dominant group, defining themselves as utterly different from the "Yahoos" (originally employees and customers of a rival company), who fled to the trackless wastes beyond the reach of the Google towers. In the Google ideology they became known as hominids and were viewed as pre-human. To the Yahoos, the Flatlanders (as those who stayed in Google Earth were called) were robots, automatons, the slaves of computer servers in Silicon Valley. Neither was regarded by the other as human, and there was some truth on both sides of that opinion. The Yahoos had degenerated into a race of bestial ruffians and louts, the Flatlanders passed their interminable lives in a robotic, almost disembodied state.

It was left to Smith and Julia to knit the two halves of the human race back together, if they could survive their ordeals.

Beast or machine? Barbarian or robot? Which would it be?

26.

When Julia was dragged out of Charrington's Antiques to be blindfolded and tossed in the back of a Customer Service van, she assumed that she was headed to a dungeon. She'd read about dungeons in the Historical Romance section of Smoky McLuggage's bookshop. They were invariably underground, dark and dank, with stone walls at least six feet thick, and crawling with rats, which she hated more than anything in the world. But when her captors arrived at their destination and dragged her inside, she found herself in the brightest, most luxurious prison she could have imagined. It looked like her idea of the bridal suite in a fancy hotel. She took a bath and went to bed, and when she awoke, a breakfast tray stood just inside the door, along with a change of clothes. The clothes seemed peculiar—a plaid kilt and knee socks—but she was grateful for a chance to change. Around noon a Yoot guard rapped on the door with his selfie stick and ushered her out to a waiting car, which drove a short distance to a shiny modern skyscraper she learned was Google Towers. In the lobby an elite squad of Yoots (their high status attested by purple hoodies, cargo shorts and glow-in-the-dark running shoes) directed her to a special elevator, in a transparent atrium, which she rode up to Higgs's penthouse.

Higgs waited smiling at the door. "Ah!" he gasped, as if he'd caught his first glimpse of a natural wonder. Julia smiled back in embarrassment, though she was no stranger to male admiration. Every man she'd ever known (admittedly they were all her cousins, except for Smith) had told her how beautiful she was, and Higgs's gasp echoed that sentiment. Her blonde hair and blue eyes—a rarity in Google Earth— seemed to excite him. Her long legs and lithesome figure added fuel to the fire, and the combination of these attractions with the schoolgirl outfit drove him wild. She knew at once that this was not the kind of innocent, detached admiration she might tolerate in a man his age. Higgs, she realized, had designs on her. That was why he made her dress up in this ridiculous costume. Since her arrest she'd been sickened by the dread of being raped by the Yoot guards, but evidently her degradation would be more subtle, though no less complete: being hit on by a snakelike, nerdy old man.

"Welcome!" Higgs said jauntily, anticipating what would happen after she'd spent a few minutes under the tin roof. "If you want to have a good time, you've come to the right place."

She laughed in his face. "Why would I come here for a good time?"

Higgs grabbed her hand and led her into the living room, where they sat on one of his six couches. Never having been in a living room with more than one couch, Julia was impressed, though not impressed enough to lie down with him, as he seemed to expect her to do. "If you're like all the other women in Google Earth," he said, "you've been bombarded all your life with WiFi waves that suppress the sex drive. But my penthouse has a special tin roof that blocks the WiFi waves and allows the pent-up natural responses of a woman to flourish, often to an extravagant degree that

wouldn't be experienced anywhere else." He tilted his head
with an air of self-regard, as if he were posing for a publicity
photo. "In a few minutes you'll be tugging me into the
bedroom."

She smiled contemptuously. "I'm surprised you don't
just handcuff me to the bed."

"I will if you want me to," Higgs said. "But you seem...
different."

"I am different. I don't need a tin roof over my head to
be a normal, fully-developed, sexually mature—"

"You're a hominid?" he gasped.

"Call me what you like. What I am is a real woman. Not
one of those sex toys you probably spend your time with."

The idea that Julia was a hominid sent Higgs's
excitement into the stratosphere. He knew she was a rebel,
and just that idea gave him a thrill, especially after he'd seen
her ascending in the elevator. She reminded him of a picture
he'd seen once—an icon in a video game made by Walt
Disney: Botticelli's *Venus*—That's who she was! How he'd
love to slide those knee socks off her willowy legs!... But
this—the revelation that she was a hominid—was almost
more than he could bear.

"I haven't lived my life under your WiFi waves," Julia
added. "I've developed normally."

"You're a natural!"

"A natural?"

"A natural woman!"

"That's right. If I love a man, that's enough to turn me
on."

Higgs could hardly control himself. "If you love a man!
If you love a man!" He jumped up and paced around the

living room self-importantly. "OK, then why not love me? All the women in the Junior Anti-Sex League love me. You can love me too. I'm CEO of the East. Last year we exceeded our profit plan by 63%, and I was compensated accordingly. And this year—"

"You think this business talk is going to turn me on?"

"Of course. It always works with women. I have more data units than any other man in Google Earth. In a few days—"

"You don't understand," Julia insisted. "Love is a feeling you either have or you don't have toward someone. You can't just decide to have it. And you can only love one person at a time."

Higgs grabbed Julia's arms and started pulling her toward the bedroom.

"Let go of me!" she shouted, prying his hands off her arms. "Sex has to be voluntary. Even if I loved you, I would still have to consent to sex."

"All right! So consent!"

"Voluntarily," she added.

This was a new idea for Higgs. Consent: OK, he got that—but *voluntary* consent? What an idea! With the tin roof, voluntary consent had never been an issue. A lesser man might have been derailed by Julia's raising it at this point in the proceedings, but Higgs was undaunted. *Au contraire,* it only inflamed his passion. Voluntary consent! The very idea drove him wild—but he had a pretty good idea how to obtain it. He had something in his tool box that no woman on Google Earth had been able to resist. It had worked on O'Brien every time: Filthy food talk!

He pulled Julia closer and started gushing in her ear: "Pizza! Hamburgers! French fries!" And now, he smiled to himself, here's the clincher: "Onion rings!"

She pried off his hands and pushed him away. "Are you nuts?"

"Tell me you love me!" he demanded.

Again she laughed in his face, more scornfully than before. "I don't love you. To be honest, I find you disgusting. No, I take that back—repulsive."

His brow darkened, and he lurched toward her, raising his hand like a weapon. "So you're just like the rest of them! You women are all alike!"

"No, I'm not," she said, backing away. "There's a man I love."

"A man you love! Who would that be?"

"His name is Smith. They captured him along with me and took him somewhere else."

Higgs laughed a hideous laugh. "I know who Smith is," he snarled. "You think you *love* that moron? Well, let me tell you something. You hominids can have your quaint customs, or instincts, or whatever they are. But you can't bring them into Google Earth. *There is no love in Google Earth!*"

"You're insane."

"Unless it's for Big Data. Or for me."

"Even more insane."

Higgs pushed a button and the Yoot guards appeared almost instantly. "Take this hominid back to her cell!"

As they led her away, he called after her: "This isn't over! I'm going to have you brought back here every day until you love me!"

27.

Smith woke up in a dim, windowless cell with no idea how long he'd been unconscious. It contained a straw pallet and a seatless toilet and nothing else. There was a small, blurry window in the door and a spigot for delivering the thin, greasy gruel that would be his only food and drink. Occasionally he peered through the window and saw the two Customer Service Representatives who'd arrested him strutting around in the corridor. Evidently this was a Customer Service prison, which was not a good sign. The straw pallet crawled with bugs; the gruel, dripping into a filthy pail, smelled like vomit. But the worst part, the part he wasn't sure he could endure, was the Hold Music. Being locked in that cell was like being on hold twenty-four hours a day, with Hold Music playing directly into his thought feed. It was obviously intended to break him.

After what seemed like days, the Hold Music stopped and a pleasant but officious woman's voice rang through the cell. "For problems with your straw pallet," the voice said, "say 'pallet.' If the problem is not enough straw, say 'insufficient straw.' If the problem is that the straw, while sufficient, is damp or mildewed, say 'smelly straw.' If the problem is that the straw, apart from being damp or mildewed, is infested with…"

The voice droned on for so long, in a seemingly infinite preview of the tortures he would endure—he lost count at eighty-eight—that he finally shouted: "Let me out of here!"

"To hear this message repeated in Urdu," the voice said, "say 'Urdu.'"

"I don't want Urdu, I just want to get out of here!"

"Current waiting time is approximately nine years, eleven months and twenty-seven days."

Suddenly Smith knew where he'd heard the voice before. It was Mrs. Lopez, the lady who'd appeared on his screen when he tried to access the Terms of Service. He struggled to keep a grip on himself: if he annoyed her, or asked to speak to her supervisor, his waiting time would go up to fifteen years.

"If the problem is with your gruel," she went on, "say 'gruel.' If the gruel has an unpleasant odor, say 'smell.' If the odor is reminiscent of—"

"Representative!" he interrupted. "I want to talk to a representative!"

"Why didn't you say so, Customer Smith?" Mrs. Lopez crooned. "A representative will be with you shortly."

Within thirty seconds the door flew open and the two Customer Service Representatives burst inside. "What seems to be the problem here?" the woman demanded.

"How long am I going to be here?"

"That totally depends on you," the man said, smiling. "You see—"

"Until your trial," the woman snarled. "And then"—she smirked at her partner—"you'll be sentenced."

"But right now," the man said, "you have a visitor."

They stepped aside respectfully, and to his amazement Smith saw O'Brien walk through the door. She carried something in her hand, hidden under a large linen napkin. When the representatives excused themselves and closed the door behind them, O'Brien snatched the napkin away like a magician performing a trick. And there on her open palm stood Smith's guppy bowl, with Mot and Derf merrily swimming side by side, wagging their little tails. "I brought your pets so you'd have someone to talk to," she said, and Smith thanked her from the bottom of his heart.

O'Brien was the last person Smith expected to meet in a Customer Service prison. When he'd seen her in *Topless Meteorologists Do Action News*, he assumed she was in the Resistance. But when Charrington turned out to work for Customer Service, he'd concluded that O'Brien had been captured and forced into cinematic prostitution. Now he realized that his assumptions about O'Brien were wildly off the mark. Here at the prison she had Customer Service Representatives opening doors for her; she could come and go as she pleased, and even bring gifts to the inmates. Running *Topless Meteorologists* back through his mind, Smith suddenly understood why. The man in the movie, whose face had appeared for just one fleeting instant, was Higgs, CEO of the East, whom Smith recognized from news streamings about the Run to Cure Narcissism.

He would have to tread carefully with O'Brien, even apart from her connection with Higgs. As his supervisor she enjoyed direct access to his thought feed. "So," he said. "How are things at Celebrity Solutions?"

"Fine," O'Brien said. Then she lowered her voice: "Trust me, Smith, I'm trying to help you."

"How can you do that?" Smith whispered.

"I have friends in high places."

"I know," Smith smiled. "I've seen the movie."

"The movie?" A furrow of concern creased O'Brien's brow. "What movie?"

"You know. *Topless Meteorologists Do Action News.* That was you and Higgs, right?"

Her face flushed to a fiery red. "He put me in a movie?"

Smith nodded. "I rented it at Charrington's."

O'Brien spat out a string of words which, Smith later learned, were commonly used only by Beast Folk. Fortunately he didn't grasp each specific word (or they might have mixed into his thought feed), but the general drift was clear enough: O'Brien regarded Higgs as the lowest form of life, significantly lower than pond scum, and from that point forward she would dedicate herself to his destruction, unless he upgraded her to Senior Management. She gave Smith no chance to respond, but instead bolted for the door and stormed past the Customer Service Representatives without another word.

When O'Brien fled, the Hold Music started up again inside Smith's head. Gruel dripped through the spigot into his pail, keeping time to the music. Bugs crawled in and out of his pallet, waving pieces of straw in time to the music. Mot and Derf wagged their little tails in time to the music. Moments came in which Smith was sure he would do anything, say anything, betray anyone if only he could make that Hold Music stop. Then he tried to get a grip on himself and remember what was important. There were two certainties in his world—he loved his pets and he loved Julia. Whatever happened, he would never betray Mot and Derf and he would never betray Julia.

Several hours—or it might have been days—passed. The lights dimmed and the music faded. He lay down on his pallet, but before he could close his eyes the cell brightened and the music blared out again, announcing a new day. There was a tap on the door and Charrington slipped inside. "Hello, Smith," he said. "I hope you're doing well. I need to ask you a few questions, if you don't mind. Your participation is completely voluntary, of course."

"That's good to know," Smith said warily.

"I mean, you haven't been tortured yet."

"No, nothing like that."

"Or beaten."

"No."

"So, as I say, this is completely voluntary." Charrington smiled at him with an air of friendly concern. "Frankly, we're a little worried about your mental health."

"We?"

"Customer Service. As you know, your thought stream has been monitored and recorded for quality control purposes for many years. And recently there have been a few specific interactions, such as when you skipped the "I am not a robot" screen—what on Google Earth were you thinking?—and the shocking things you said at the antique shop. You know, about Goldstein and all that. No one in his right mind would say such things to Customer Service."

"But you're the one who gave me the Goldstein video!" Smith objected, confident that he could defend himself against such an illogical accusation. "And you didn't tell me you worked for Customer Service!"

"It's not like we're trying to trip you up, Smith, or set traps for you or anything like that. This is Customer Service. We're here to help you."

"OK," Smith nodded. The one thing he remembered about the Terms of Service was that you couldn't argue with Customer Service. "I know that."

"It's your mental health we're concerned about, not what you say or do," Charrington smiled. "We want you to be happy. But something you said at the antique shop was highly troubling, as a glimpse into your mental state. It gave the impression that you don't love Big Data. So I'll ask you point blank: Do you love Big Data?"

Smith felt trapped. Under the Terms of Service, as he recalled, the only offense worse than arguing with Customer Service was attempting to deceive them ("attempting" was the key word, since successful deception was impossible). Thus, although he couldn't deny what he'd said at the antique shop, neither could he appear to conveniently change his mind in response to Charrington's pressure. "Sure, I love Big Data," he said. "I just don't think it's infallible, that's all."

Charrington found this tactic amusing. "How's your memory, Smith?" he asked. "Pretty good? OK, what color socks was O'Brien wearing when she was here this morning?"

"I don't remember," Smith said. "The color of her socks wasn't important."

"Not important, eh? OK, let's see how good your memory is for important things. Here's one you should know. There was an important sacrifice two weeks ago. What celebrities were sacrificed?"

"That's easy. Justin Bleeper and Smiley Cirrus. I handled the publicity."

"Is that your final answer?"

"Absolutely."

"Then let's do a Google search." Charrington furrowed his brow with an air of deep concentration. "Ah!" he exclaimed with mock surprise. "The Google search reveals that it was not Justin Bleeper and Smiley Cirrus at all. It was Scarlatina Johnnson and Lady GooGoo."

"No, that's wrong, I remember very clearly—"

"You must be mistaken. Big Data is never wrong."

"No, I'm sure I'm right."

"Here's the problem, Smith." Charrington laid a hand on Smith's shoulder and looked him in the eye, imploring him to listen to reason. "As between your memory and a Google search, which one do you expect me to believe? Your memory is a function of your brain—four pounds of outmoded neural cells with a random access memory below that of the average coffee maker. And where does a Google search go? To the Geniuses at Nusquama University, who look up the answer in Wonkapaedia. Which one do you think I should believe?"

"You have a point," Smith conceded, trying to sound reasonable. "But in this case"—he had to stand his ground or Charrington would lose all respect for him—"I'm totally sure it was Justin Bleeper and Smiley Cirrus."

"Come on, Smith! If you have a question, what do you do? You Google it. But now you tell me that in just this one instance, this one special case in the entire history of the universe—the identity of the celebrities who were thrown to the lions two weeks ago in a public sacrifice—we should rely on your memory, which can't even tell us what color socks O'Brien was wearing this morning!"

28.

O'Brien was incensed at what Smith had told her about *Topless Meteorologists Do Action News*. If Smith could be believed, Higgs was filming their encounters and renting out the videos to perverts in antique shops. But just how far could she trust Smith? At Celebrity Solutions he'd always seemed a likeable moron; now he was in Customer Service custody, apparently a follower of Goldstein. Should she believe him? Was Higgs just using her as a sex toy? Was she just one of his many mistresses? The only way to find out was to continue the repulsive relationship. It gave her a sense of power, if nothing else. She intended to use it to force Higgs to upgrade her to Senior Management.

At her next visit Higgs was unusually passionate, murmuring business talk in her ear even before he dragged her into the bedroom. "You're a doll!" he said, smiling into her eyes.

"Before we get started," she said, "there's something we need to discuss. Do you remember saying that if I gave you what you wanted, I'd be upgraded to Senior Management?"

"Remember?" he laughed. "What does that mean?"

"It was about six weeks ago—"

"Have you ever noticed that everything's always new, but nothing ever changes?" he interrupted. "There's a reason for that. Every byte of data in the servers—except the algorithms and the core functions that keep Senior Management in control—is deleted after thirty days. If you think you remember something longer than that, you must be mistaken."

She felt wobbly and desperate now as he took her by the hand and led her toward the bedroom. "There's nothing wrong with your memory," he said. "It's just that for you there's nothing to remember that's more than thirty days old—nothing real, that is, as recorded on the servers. Virtual reality is the only reality."

In the bedroom, she made a glancing search for hidden cameras. Finding none, she sat on the bed and started to pull off her knee socks. "Let me do that!" he insisted, reaching for her ankle.

"You said I'd be upgraded," she said, blocking his hand.

"And you will be." She started to speak but he stopped her words with a kiss. "And when you're initiated into Senior Management, you'll have access to memories that go back much farther than thirty days. You'll be indoctrinated in the secret tradition, passed down from one level of Senior Management to another, that records the history of Google Earth. If eventually you reach the thirty-third degree, as I have, you'll know everything there is to know, and you'll understand how all the pieces fit together."

Higgs slipped off both knee socks and stroked O'Brien's ankles. "In the beginning," he said, his passion rising as he gave her a tantalizing glimpse of the secret doctrine, "the worldwide web was chaotic and without form, free and open to all. Millions of products contended on the web—you could search for them on Google and buy them on Amazon. Most of those products were useless, wasteful, overpriced, even downright harmful, but the customer had the freedom to choose among them, even if it meant choosing the worst over the best.

"Ironically"—Higgs sucked in a breath to give special emphasis to that word—"that freedom, expressing itself in a trillion actual choices, was what enabled Big Data, after recording those choices and reducing them to algorithms, infallibly to make the one right choice for all times in every product category. People no longer needed to know about products that were useless, wasteful, or overpriced—they only needed to know which one was the *best*, the one that would bring the greatest happiness to the greatest number."

Breathless now, Higgs had O'Brien completely in his power, carried away by his violent motions, the intoxication of his business talk and the prospect of initiation into Senior Management—or so she made it seem. In fact she felt as cold as a slab of bacon, and all her writhings and expostulations were but a simulacrum—the human equivalent of a computer simulation—of the emotions Higgs thought he was arousing in her. "Virtual reality is the only reality!" she repeated to herself.

"Google," Higgs gushed on, "which had thrived on the multiplicity of choices, could see the day of reckoning ahead: the day when only one choice would be possible or permissible. By the time of the Great Stench, Google knew that, if it wanted to survive, it would have to be a monopoly. It bought up all the other companies—Amazon, Fakebook, Twitter, Apple, Microsoft, Walt Disney, Monsanto—and created the empire known as Google Earth. No longer would customers live at the mercy of a million marketing schemes. No longer would they be bombarded day and night with idiotic advertising and annoying promotional messages. They would still have the freedom to choose, but there would be only one choice: the choice determined by Big Data!"

Higgs was probably the only man in Google Earth who punctuated his amorous encounters with bullet points from a PowerPoint presentation, each emphasized by an energetic jab of the pointer. "Today," he panted, "there's only one brand in each category:

- *One* search engine: Google—because every search has only one right answer, and Google provides it.

- *One* retailer: Amazon—because there's only one product that's best for you, and Amazon provides it.

- *One* restaurant: McDonalds—because there's only one way to serve GMO desiccated carbohydrate cubes, and McDonalds provides it."

"Yes!" O'Brien agreed, hoping that Ralph (though admittedly a Yes Man) would refrain from chiming in.

Higgs seemed to be reaching the moment of truth. "There's no past and no future, only the eternal present!"

"Yes!" O'Brien repeated.

"Who controls the algorithms controls the world!" Higgs bellowed. He clasped his hands around O'Brien's throat and started choking her. When she pushed him back he tightened his grip and leaned down hard as he continued his deranged monologue. "Is there still choice in this world? Of course there is!" he shouted with the ecstasy of madness in his eyes. "Obedience is Choice!"

Mission accomplished, he rolled aside and lay on his back as O'Brien struggled to catch her breath. "Believe it or not," Higgs said, "there are still people who rebel against Big Data and want to turn the clock back to the days before the Great Stench. People who want the right to choose evil (in my opinion that's not too strong a word for products that aren't endorsed by *Consumer Reports*) and who think having the right to make that choice marks them as morally superior to everyone else."

Within a few seconds Higgs was asleep and snoring raucously. O'Brien leaned across his chest and whispered into his EyeWatch. "Pssst! Ralph! Are you there!"

"Where else would I be?"

"Thanks for keeping quiet this time. That other time, when you spoke up—"

"Sorry about that," Ralph said. "Hey, is this guy as big of an ass as he sounds?"

"Way bigger." O'Brien kept her eyes on Higgs's face to make sure he was still asleep. "Listen, I've got to ask you something. Did Higgs make a movie when I was here one other time?"

Ralph laughed, if an EyeWatch could be said to laugh. It came out more like a dry electronic crackle. "He films everything. Then he has some intern Photoshop the videos together with different women in them so he can picture himself as a porn star."

O'Brien felt her breath tightening as her blood pressure rose. If she ever got Higgs alone on the rooftop, near the railing....

"There's a new girl he's after," Ralph said, adding fuel to the flames. "He calls her Julia. She's driving him wild because she won't go to bed with him."

"Why not? Doesn't she come to the penthouse?"

"She says she doesn't need a tin roof over her head, but she still refuses to sleep with him. Higgs calls her a natural, whatever that means."

"A natural? What does that make me?"

"He says you're just a wind-up doll, an automaton without a soul. The only things you're good for are sex, making coffee and sending out tweets."

For O'Brien it was a close call whether to strangle Higgs with his shoe laces, disembowel him with his corkscrew or unman him with his electric sushi knife. While considering her options, she jumped out of bed and started stretching and tearing her clothes as she tried to pull them on.

"There's something else you should know," Ralph said. "Higgs is planning to kill everybody. The entire human race. He says they're overdue for extinction."

"Extinction? Is that...?"

"Yeah," Ralph said. "The Next Big Thing."

29.

Now the Hold Music never stopped, even when Smith was sleeping. Whenever the dripping gruel filled his pail three-quarters full, he forced himself to swallow it. After he'd done that three times, he scratched the wall with his fingernail to mark off another day. Then he shook the bugs out of his pallet and slept until they came back and took enough bites to wake him up. Five days passed in this fashion before Charrington returned, noticeably less amiable than before. He made it clear that he was still unhappy with Smith's insistence on knowing more than Google. "Has there always been a Sea of Shells?" he asked Smith.

"I don't think so," Smith said. "I think there used to be something there called the Atlantic Ocean."

"How do you know that?"

"I just know it, that's all."

"Did you learn that through a Google search? I doubt it very much, because I just checked Wonkapaedia, which says the Sea of Shells has always been there. Do you dispute that?"

Smith lowered his eyes and turned away. "It's not what I remember."

With a hand on his chin, Charrington twisted Smith's head back around and forced him to lift his eyes. "We care about you here, Smith," he said. "We want you to be happy, and this is highly disturbing. Obviously you are mentally deranged. You remember things that didn't happen, and you don't remember things that did happen. That's what's known as a delusion."

"All right," Smith said. "The Sea of Shells has always been there. Scarlatina Johnnson and Lady GooGoo were sacrificed two weeks ago. Can I go now?"

"You're lying, Smith. You don't believe a word of what you just said."

"I can't change what I believe just by wishing that the facts were different."

"No, of course not."

"There's such a thing as a fact. You can't trick yourself into believing something you know isn't true."

"No, of course not." Charrington's voice sounded cold now, as if his patience was exhausted. "But if you persist in believing and asserting things that are contrary to the objective results of a Google search, you'll pardon us for wondering if you love Big Data."

"I do love Big Data," Smith insisted. He wasn't lying: after all he'd been through, he still couldn't imagine a world without Big Data watching over him. "Honestly, I do."

"But you think you know better than Big Data. You think you're smarter than Big Data."

"No, I don't."

Charrington flashed a fake smile—fake and obviously intended to be perceived as fake—so there could be no doubt that what followed would be Smith's last chance. "Then let me ask you again: Has the Sea of Shells always been there?"

Smith turned his eyes away and refused to answer.

"Which Celebrities were sacrificed two weeks ago?"

Smith said nothing.

"I know what you're thinking," Charrington said. "I always know what you're thinking. You're thinking Justin Bleeper and Smiley Cirrus were sacrificed but maybe you'll say Scarlatina Johnnson and Lady GooGoo because that's what I want to hear. But you see, Smith, that misses the point. I'm not trying to get you to say something you don't believe. I want you to be *right.*"

Abruptly, he pivoted and walked out the door, returning about thirty seconds later. "Do you love Julia?" he asked.

"Yes," Smith said.

"Does she love you?"

"Yes. I hope she does. I know she does."

"Come with me," Charrington smirked. "I want to show you something."

He led Smith into the corridor, where the two Customer Service Representatives stood to one side, also smirking. From the other end of the hall Smith could hear a chorus of hysterical screaming, as if people were being beaten in one of the rooms. "What's going on in there?" he demanded.

"Just a customer focus group," Charrington said. "They're suspected of brand disloyalty."

He opened another door and led Smith into a conference room equipped with a wall-sized screen. "Have a seat."

Charrington clicked on the TV and a video flashed on the screen. It was a movie similar to *Topless Meteorologists Do Action News*, only this time it took place in a bedroom and there was no effort to hide the man's face. It was Higgs, hissing filthy food talk into the ear of the woman, who was clearly enjoying herself. Though at first her face was hidden, she seemed somehow familiar. Was it O'Brien again? No, this woman had blonde hair, and—No! It couldn't be!

Smith retched and nearly lost consciousness when he realized that the woman was Julia.

O'Brien arranged to meet Bumstead in the Junior Anti-Sex League cafeteria, where—ironically, as Higgs might have said—they shared a pitcher of Kool Aid. In a quiet voice, so as not to be overheard by the Beast Folk who were clearing the tables, she related what Ralph had told her about the Next Big Thing.

"Extinction?" Bumstead gasped. "Did I hear you right?"

"Yes," O'Brien said. "The entire human race—except, presumably, himself."

"He's putting his solipsism into practice." Bumstead's eyes narrowed. "Are you sure about this?"

"I got it from the horse's mouth—Higgs's EyeWatch."

"You talk to Higgs's EyeWatch?"

"Trust me, Ralph hates him as much as I do."

"How is he going to pull it off?" Bumstead asked.

"I'm not clear on the details," O'Brien said. "All I know is that he wants me to send out some tweets tomorrow from the Message Center, directing everyone to converge on the Stadium the next day."

"For the big Celebrity sacrifice?"

"Supposedly it's for that, and the Run to Cure Narcissism, but Ralph told me it's also for the Next Big Thing. There's this new slogan—"

"Find Your Future In The Cloud," Bumstead muttered.

"That's right. That's one of the tweets I'm supposed to send out."

"The Board of Directors approved that. We thought it was just another meaningless marketing slogan."

"It means everyone is going to the Cloud," O'Brien said. "Not just the Celebrities."

It was the night before Smith's trial. He'd hardly touched his gruel since the last interrogation, when Charrington showed him the video of Julia with Higgs. He no longer cared how much the bugs in his pallet bit him, or how many days he'd been in prison. Even the incessant Hold Music—Mrs. Lopez had advised him that current waiting time was now approximately ten years, three months and six days—had lost its sting. Nothing could torment him more than the ordinary procession of moments in his life. Even Mot and Derf, cute as they were, couldn't salve his despair. Without Julia, life was not worth living.

Charrington smiled as he glided through the door. "We're going to resume these sessions, at an enhanced level, after your trial," he told Smith. "The trial is a formality. You'll be convicted and sentenced, and then you'll be dealing with Customer Service for a long time to come, until you understand that Big Data says what reality is. Not you, not I, not Customer Service. Big Data. There's no escape. And don't bother confessing unless you believe what you say. You have free will—you're a man, not a machine—but the only rational use of that free will is to surrender yourself to the superior power of Big Data. Obedience is Choice. Freedom is Connectivity."

Smith stared blankly ahead, indifferent to Charrington and anything he could say or do. He agreed that the trial would be a formality. It would have no impact on him. Without Julia, his life was over.

"It's important that you understand the charges against you," Charrington said. "For the past couple of weeks, your thought feed has been seething with unauthorized words and phrases. One of the worst violations involves thinking about 'Life, Liberty and the pursuit of Happiness.'"

Charrington's face was glowing red. Until then, he had humored Smith with an air of benevolent patience. Now, for the first time, he seemed to be angry. "Don't you realize that you already have as much happiness as it is possible to have?" he shouted. "No 'liberty' is required so you can 'pursue' the chimera of *more* happiness. Big Data has given us the greatest liberty ever afforded to human beings since time began. Our minds and bodies signal what we need and it is ours. Since Big Data knows everything that can be known about each product and each customer, the match-up is instantaneous and perfect, eliminating the inefficiencies of advertising, shopping, retail stores, salesmanship. Can't you see that?"

As Charrington spoke, the little voice that Smith had come to depend on emerged quietly from the hiss of the thought feed. "Don't give up!" it said. "Don't give up on Liberty and the pursuit of Happiness!" Smith steeled his nerves for resistance. "I watched the Goldstein video you gave me," he said. "Goldstein says, 'You can do whatever you want.' That's what Liberty is."

Charrington laughed in his face. "Do you know what Goldstein doesn't tell his followers? He doesn't tell them that if they follow him, they face a future of pain, endless toil, suffering and death. Is that what you want? Do you even know what death is?"

"I don't care. All I know is, I can do whatever I want."

Charrington shook his head as if suddenly taking pity on Smith. "I gave you that video," he said, "and now I'm going to let you in on a little secret. Goldstein doesn't exist. He's a figment of Big Data's imagination, the projection of what evil would be if it could exist."

"That's a lie."

"There's no good and evil in Google Earth. Don't look for escape in joining the battle between some mythical opposition of forces, or transcending some dichotomy that doesn't exist. Big Data is all there is."

He reached out and touched Smith's arm, flashing a warm smile to show his concern. "Smith, try to believe me," he said. "I'm on your side. You don't need to die if you love Big Data with all your heart. Even the Terms of Service hang on that general principle. Now what does that mean, to love Big Data with all your heart? It means *there can be no room left in your heart to love anyone else.* And that includes pets and women. So let me ask you: Do you love Big Data with all your heart?"

"Yes," Smith replied woodenly.

Charrington paused and stared into his eyes. "Do you love Julia?"

"No," Smith lied. He realized that the only way he could go on loving Julia was to deny that he loved her. "I don't love Julia, but I do love my pets."

"Do you mean these two little guppies?"

"Yes."

Charrington lifted the bowl and beamed down on the guppies. "Mot and Derf, I believe you call them." And with a sudden motion he lunged to one side, dumped out the tank and flushed Mot and Derf down the toilet.

30

On the morning of his trial, Smith was led by the Yoot guards into a windowless conference room to sit across a table from his court-assigned attorney, a small, nervous man named Quarke who'd never tried a case before. In fact, Quarke had graduated from law school just two days earlier, where his major, as with all lawyers in Google Earth, had been intellectual property law. This course of study (conducted online at UNEWVAK) had not been especially challenging—intellectual property was the only kind of property in Google Earth, and it all belonged to Google—but the only other subject offered was contract law, focusing on the Terms of Service, which, per Google policy, Quarke had not been allowed to read. With this superb education fresh in mind, Quarke was well-qualified to provide Smith with the zealous representation to which he was entitled—so it was said—under the Terms of Service. Smith, for his part, felt coldly indifferent to his own fate. After losing Julia and then Mot and Derf, he knew there was nothing the Customer Service Court could do to make his life any worse.

Quarke began by explaining the charges against Smith and their potential consequences. Unfortunately, he was so punctilious about the protection of Google's intellectual property that his speech was unintelligible. When a word was followed by the small circled "R" that indicates a registered trademark, he would end the word with a growl, and when it was followed by the "TM" superscript that signifies an unregistered trademark, he would conclude with an explosion followed by a gulp, and if the word was subject to copyright (as all words in English® were) he wouldn't finish the word until he'd twisted his tongue in a complete circle around the letter "C"—with the overall effect, after all the tics and clicks and growls were sprinkled into each sentence, of a Xhosa-speaking Tourette's victim conducting a séance with Edward G. Robinson. "In Google Earth-*rrrr!*," he told Smith, "where we speak English-*rrrr!*, except in Canada-*t-t-t-t-mmmm* where they also speak French-*t-t-t-t-mmmm*, all words including Life, *see?* Liberty, *see?* and Happiness, *see?* are Copyright, *see?* by Google Inc."

"I can't understand a word you're saying," Smith protested.

"All right, I'll leave out the copyright and trademark symbols, subject to your agreement, incorporated herein by reference, that English-*rrrr!*—sorry!—is a registered trademark of Google Inc. and all English words are subject to Google's copyright."

"OK, I agree," Smith said.

Quarke shuffled through a stack of papers and looked his client in the eye. "You're charged with a list of serious crimes that carry lengthy sentences," he said. "Making a false or misleading statement to Customer Service — 25 years. Failing to implement a suggestion by Customer Service — 25 years. Hanging up on Customer Service — 25 years."

He flipped ahead as if skipping over the less serious offenses. "And then there are the copyright violations," he said. "Apparently you tried to read something called the

Declaration of Independence, which includes copyrighted words and phrases not covered in your license."

"I did read it," Smith admitted. "I even memorized it. I also read—"

Quarke cut him off before he could make any more incriminating statements. "Unlicensed use of copyrighted words—20 years for each violation, which means each time you used the word or even thought about using it. And then there are the enabling crimes: Getting up in the morning to commit copyright infringement — 10 years per violation. Breathing while in the act of copyright infringement — 10 years per violation. Introducing unlicensed mental impressions into the thought feed — 10 years per violation. By my calculation, you're looking at 2,346 years for the copyright violations alone."

Smith leaped up and paced in front of the table. "What happens during all these years?" he cried. "Are you talking about prison?" The idea of spending 2,346 years in a Customer Service prison was more than he could bear.

"Prison?" Quarke exclaimed. "You should be so lucky! They're going to put you on hold—with Hold Music twenty-four hours a day—and reduce your data allotment to a level where you won't be able to form a coherent thought. Even if you're allowed to stay in your condo, your life won't be worth living."

"Don't I have any defenses?"

"Yes, certainly. That's what I'm here for. My advice is to plead insanity."

Smith was incredulous. "Plead insanity for copyright infringement?"

"It's your only hope."

"Can't I plea bargain or something?"

"Yes, of course. I was coming to that." Quarke thumbed through the papers until he came to an official-looking document. "The District Attorney has offered to let you plead guilty to first-degree murder, aggravated assault, grand larceny, treason and insider trading."

"But I didn't commit any of those crimes!"

"That doesn't matter when you're plea bargaining. You can plead guilty to anything you want."

Smith sat down and buried his head in his hands. "I won't plead guilty to something I didn't do."

"You've got it all backwards, Smith," Quarke scoffed. "Do you think the District Attorney would accept a guilty plea for something you actually did? What good would that do him, when he can put you on trial and convict you in fifteen minutes? But if you *didn't* commit the crime—well, that's a different story, isn't it? Quite a feather in his cap if he scores a conviction on that one!"

Smith pounded the table hopelessly. "But I shouldn't be convicted of a crime I didn't commit!"

"The DA won't consider a plea unless you accept the maximum sentence," Quarke went on brightly, "which is what I recommend. The maximum sentence for all the crimes he wants you to plead guilty to is only 1,984 years. You'll be back on the street in no time."

Against Quarke's advice, Smith declined the offer to plead guilty to first-degree murder, aggravated assault, grand larceny, treason and insider trading. Surely, he reasoned, what he'd done was less serious than any of those crimes, and when the jury heard the evidence they would grasp the injustice of the case against him, when all he'd done was try to think independently—admittedly in English, he wouldn't try to deny that—and access the Terms of Service. He envisioned himself, when it came his turn to testify, standing up to deliver a stirring recitation of the Declaration of Independence, which he'd memorized during his stay in the crypt. But as it happened, his image of a criminal trial—gleaned from old hominid movies starring Spencer Tracy or Paul Newman—was wildly off the mark.

The District Attorney, whose name was Furlowe, was a tall, angular man with a blotchy complexion. His face looked lopsided, as if it had come out of a malfunctioning 3-D printer, giving him the advantage of having two different faces, either of which he could deploy at will. He wore an absurd costume consisting of charcoal gray trousers and a matching jacket, both etched with faint vertical stripes, and a long swatch of yellow silk dangling from his neck across the front of his white shirt, which was buttoned tightly at the collar. In spite of that outlandish outfit he seemed vain about his appearance, aiming the good-natured, likeable side of his face to the cameras as he strutted around fist–bumping the news reporters and camera operators, and pointing the nasty, vindictive side only at Smith and Quarke.

The courtroom — a high-ceilinged room reminiscent of a school gymnasium — had a carnival atmosphere, notwithstanding the Yoot bailiffs who stood around its perimeter, shouting and shaking their selfie sticks in an effort to quiet the crowd. Smith saw Charrington and the two Customer Service Representatives who'd arrested him in the back row, joking with one of the news reporters, and O'Brien sitting beside them, seemingly lost in her own thoughts. And to his surprise he noticed the Beast Folk he'd befriended at the Stadium, handing out desiccated protein patties and starch chips at the refreshment stand in their McDonalds uniforms. Between the audience and the judge's bench stood two tables, a teak conference table for the prosecution and a folding aluminum card table for the defense. A jury box containing twelve empty seats stretched along one wall, and a giant TV screen occupied the other. Furlowe took his seat at the prosecution table, snarling in Smith's direction as he smiled toward the cameras with the other side of his face. "Your trial is being streamed all over Google Earth as an example to others," he told Smith. "Does it remind you of anything?"

Yes it did, Smith realized with a sinking sensation. It reminded him of a Celebrity sacrifice.

31.

"All rise!" the Yoot bailiffs shouted in unison. As everyone in the courtroom leaped to their feet, Customer Service Judge Grimsby slinked in from a little door behind the bench and slipped into her seat. The part of her that was visible to Smith—essentially her eyebrows and the top of her head—resembled a small furry animal lying on its side and twitching occasionally. After a certain amount of paper rustling, she aimed her eyebrows at Furlowe and pounded her gavel. "Is the prosecution ready to proceed? I don't have all day."

Furlowe strode to the lectern and introduced himself as the District Attorney for the Eastern District of Google Earth, Nusquama Division. He then asked the court to enter a verdict of guilty on all counts.

Quarke immediately rose to object. "Smith is entitled to be tried by a jury of his peers," he said in a high, squeaky voice, pointing to the empty jury box. "Where are they?"

Judge Grimsby leaned forward, possibly in order to give the cameras a better view of her face. "The jury is in the jury room, where they will be sequestered until they reach a verdict."

"A verdict? But they haven't heard the evidence yet!"

The judge and Furlowe exchanged a smirk, not without sympathy for the novice attorney. Quarke had committed the kind of *faux pas* you might expect from a lawyer trying his first case. "The jurors are ordinary citizens," Judge Grimsby explained patiently. "Obviously they can't be given access to the kind of top secret information that's needed to prove the serious crimes Smith has committed. And even if they were, they wouldn't understand it."

"But—"

"We confirmed that during jury selection, Your Honor," Furlowe jumped in. "The average juror on this panel, like the average member of the public—and I would remind Quarke that the defendant is entitled to a jury of his peers, not a jury of geniuses with a high security clearance—is limited to 50 data units per message." He paused to emphasize this disturbing fact. "Idiots, in other words. They probably can't remember their own names."

"Then how can you expect them to understand the evidence?" Quarke demanded, in a tone of triumph.

"Precisely the point!" Furlowe said. "At the 50-unit level of comprehension, not a single juror would be able to understand the evidence in this case. *If*"—he turned his good side toward the cameras and paused again, having saved the clincher for last—"*If,* that is, there were going to *be* any evidence."

The crowd loosed a volley of jeers and catcalls, apparently aimed at Smith. "Which there is not," the judge said, banging her gavel. "I've already decided that."

"On what basis, Your Honor?" Quarke squeaked, glaring at the crowd.

"There are no facts in dispute." Judge Grimsby scowled at Quarke for wasting her time. "Let's get on with the trial. I don't have all day."

She banged her gavel again and the trial began.

In his penthouse, Higgs watched Smith's trial on his screen with an acute personal interest, informed by jealousy. Julia, the natural woman who'd excited him as no female had before, claimed to love Smith with all her heart. This Higgs found hard to believe. Everyone who knew Smith, including O'Brien, agreed that he was a moron, and nothing Higgs saw at the trial had altered that impression. "How could Julia give this man the time of day?" he muttered to himself. "I could print out a better man on my 3-D printer!"

That gave Higgs an idea. After the Next Big Thing, he'd often wondered, what would he do for an encore? Now he knew: He could use his 3-D printer to fashion a whole new human race!

The big event was scheduled for the next day, and things were falling nicely into place. The Olympic diving tank had been completed and filled with water, with fifty-gallon drums of pink Kool Aid powder standing ready to be stirred in. Dozens of small spigots had been installed near the bottom of the tank, poised to fill thousands of small plastic cups. The "secret ingredient" (a secret to everyone but Higgs, who would add it to the Kool Aid at the last minute) had arrived in his latest Amazon shipment. Surprisingly, even though ten pounds of the stuff was sufficient to exterminate the entire human race, Monsanto offered a "Buy 10 Pounds, Get Another 10 Pounds Free!" special. Higgs had ordered twenty pounds, just to be on the safe side. At an average cost of only 60 data units per pound, how could you go wrong?

An anxious announcer broke into the news feed with images of a dramatic Celebrity break under the Stadium. Bob Dillweed, strumming a guitar, could be seen leading an army of rebellious Celebrities as they emerged from the

Substadium into the street, mobbed by fans and paparazzi, less than a block from the Customer Service Courthouse where Smith was on trial. "These are hardened publicity hounds," the announcer said, "who have escaped from their pens the day before they're scheduled to be sacrificed. The authorities are doing everything possible to restore order."

A small cadre of elite Yoot guards, in their purple hoodies, cargo shorts and glow-in-the-dark running shoes, struggled to control the crowd with their selfie sticks. Higgs noticed some familiar faces among the rebels—Linsey Lowhand, Kam Kardashiam and even Arnold Schnortzensnickers, who hadn't been seen since the last of the "Service Terminator" movies about a Customer Service Representative sent back from the future to terminate the service of Google customers who lied about the names of their first pets. Kam Kardashiam, her mask-like smile hardened by years of plastic surgery and Botox injections, pushed forward through the crowd brandishing her Diamond Dream Stilettos, while Linsey Lowhand threatened to douse the Yoot guards' hoodies with nail polish remover.

"Not to walk on all fours!" Arnold Schnortzensnickers growled. "That is the law!"

Linsey Lowhand rolled her eyes plaintively over the crowd. "Not to shoplift on Rodeo Drive!" she shouted. "That is the law!"

Higgs laughed out loud. "Do you hear that, Ralph?" he asked his watch. "It's as if they're trying to sound human. How pathetic!"

"Yes," Ralph agreed.

"Not to take selfies twenty-four hours a day!" Kam Kardashiam moaned. "That is the law!"

The Yoot guards pulled their hoodies down around their faces and surged forward into the crowd.

As the battle raged, the news feed switched back to Smith's trial, which had continued its inexorable course with the full majesty of the law, heedless of the ignorant armies clashing in the streets outside. "The Copyright Act of 2084," Furlowe was saying, "codified the exclusive rights Google had obtained under the Terms of Service, which everyone in the world accepted."

Judge Grimsby frowned. *"Everyone in the world?"*

"Yes, Your Honor," Furlowe said. "Literally everyone in the world, including the French, who ordinarily won't agree to anything, accepted the Terms of Service. We have the records to prove it."

Quarke leaped to his feet. "Your Honor, the sordid history of how Google took over the world by inducing people to accept its Terms of Service—"

"This isn't the time for speeches, counselor," the judge interrupted. She nodded at Furlowe. "Proceed."

"Thank you, Your Honor. Let me just reiterate that under the Terms of Service, each and every one of the protections now codified in the Copyright Act was specifically agreed to *by the entire population of Google Earth.* That includes Smith."

"Objection, Your Honor!" Quarke's voice trembled with indignation. "All this happened long before Smith even existed. How could he have agreed to such restrictions?"

"Very simple," Furlowe smiled. "One of the Terms of Service has always been that Google reserves the right to *modify, alter or amend the Terms of Service at any time,* and any amendment will be binding on the user, *and his or her heirs, successors and assigns, forever.*

"And since the entire population of Google Earth agreed to the Terms of Service, it stands to reason that Smith is bound by them. He must be the heir, successor or assign of *someone* who agreed to the restrictions."

Quarke, who had started to object, sank dejectedly into his seat. Furlowe's logic was unassailable.

"Proceed," said the judge.

"Thank you, Your Honor. Now, with the court's permission, I will cite the portions of the Copyright Act that spell out the charges against Smith." Furlowe jabbed his finger toward the huge wall screen and a PowerPoint slide flashed into view, with certain passages of the Copyright Act highlighted in a bold, vivid font. *"As to any copyright recognized by this Act,"* he read aloud, *"it shall be an infringement of such copyright*——I'll just skip over the irrelevant verbiage, with the court's permission."

"Come to the point!" the judge snapped. "I don't have all day."

"... for any person, without a valid license from the copyright holder—the copyright holder in this case being Google, Your Honor—"

"Of course it's Google. Who else could it be?"

"Precisely, Your Honor," Furlowe smiled. *"It shall be an infringement of such copyright for any person"*—That would include the defendant, Smith—*"to form a mental impression"*—Those are the four key words, Your Honor: 'form a mental impression;' I can't emphasize those words enough—*"of any word or expression not covered by the applicable license or containing in excess of the maximum number of data units authorized to such user under the applicable license."*

"Gibberish!" the judge observed.

"Yes, of course, Your Honor. Nevertheless it is the law."

Judge Grimsby's eyes narrowed as she aimed them at Furlowe. "You keep emphasizing the words 'mental impression.' What does that phrase mean?"

"A 'mental impression' is what in common parlance is known as a *thought*. In other words, it's unlawful to have a thought that includes unlicensed words or exceeds the licensed number of data units."

Satisfied with this answer, the judge settled back in her chair and nodded toward the defendant's table. "Quarke? Do you have anything to say?"

"I certainly do, Your Honor," Quarke chirped, springing to his feet. "This trial is a sham, a mockery and—"

"Objection!" Furlowe shouted. "Quarke is not licensed to use those words. Are you, Quarke? Does your license include 'sham' or 'mockery' when used to describe legal proceedings?"

"No," Quarke admitted sheepishly.

"And unless I'm very much mistaken, the next word you were going to say was 'farce,' was it not?"

"Yes, it was. That's what this is, a sham, a mockery and a—"

Furlowe stamped his foot. "You can't call it a farce! And you can't call it a travesty either! Or a travesty of a sham and a mockery and a farce!"

"Proceed," the judge admonished

"Your Honor," Quarke said, "it's ironic—"

"Objection to the word 'ironic'!"

"Overruled! Let's get this over with! I don't have all day!"

"It's ironic"—Quarke glared defiantly at Furlowe—"ironic, to say the least, that my client stands accused of a crime involving thought. Smith has never been a deep thinker, or any kind of thinker, for that matter. In fact, most people who know him—including his supervisor, O'Brien—consider him a moron. The infringement he's accused of concerns a passage from the Declaration of Independence—"

"Objection! The Declaration of Independence has been superseded by the Terms of Service."

"We don't dispute that, Your Honor," Quarke conceded. "Smith apparently found a copy of that ancient document and tried to understand a sentence in it, which, admittedly, is 208 data units long. He couldn't make any sense of that sentence, although he did succeed in memorizing it. He has diminished capacity, hence lack of criminal intent—"

"You're not licensed to raise those defenses!"

Judge Grimsby had lost her patience with Quarke. "I'm afraid your arguments are inadmissible, Quarke. And may I remind you: I don't have all day! Sit down!" Quarke slid into his chair beside Smith, his hand trembling as he jotted a note on his legal pad.

Smith glanced up to find the judge glowering at him over the edge of the bench. "Is it true that you were trying to understand a passage from the Declaration of Independence?" she demanded.

"Yes, Your Honor," Smith said, rising to his feet. "And with all due respect, I think I do understand it." He gazed around the courtroom and waited until all eyes were upon him. *"We hold these truths to be self-evident, that all men are created equal, that they are endowed by their Creator with certain unalienable Rights, that among these are Life, Liberty, and the pursuit of Happiness."*

Pandemonium broke out in the courtroom when Smith said *the pursuit of Happiness*. Furlowe howled "Objection!" and pounded the table. "Suppress the witness!" the judge yelled, banging her gavel. Bailiffs came running in from all directions and piled on top of Smith, clamping their grip on his wrists and ankles and wrestling him into a twisted tangle on the floor.

When order had been restored, Judge Grimsby climbed up on her chair so she could peer down at Smith, who was barely visible under all the bailiffs that were still actively suppressing him. "Smith," she intoned, "the jury will be directed to enter a verdict of guilty on all counts. You have used unauthorized words to form mental impressions in excess of your data license. Moreover, in forming the mental impression *the pursuit of Happiness,* you are guilty of the crimes of customer dissatisfaction, subversion and treason."

The judge raised her gavel as she prepared to impose the sentence. "Your data allotment will be reduced to the minimum amount necessary to pay for around-the-clock Hold Music," she said, "for the rest of your natural life. Customer Service will be directed to implement this change at once. Any further violations may result in Termination of Service. Do you understand? Termination of Service!"

Smith wrenched himself free of the bailiffs and staggered to his feet as Judge Grimsby brought her gavel down for the last time. "The Court is adjourned!"

32.

At the very instant Smith's sentence was announced, a clamor arose in the back of the courtroom and the bailiffs rushed over to suppress it. The escaped Celebrities, led by Bob Dillweed, had overcome the Yoot guards and marched into the Customer Service Courthouse. As if on cue, the Beast Folk manning the McDonalds refreshment stand broke into a chorus of "We ain't gonna work on Big Mackie's farm no more!" and joined the protest. The spectators, followed by the bailiffs and the Yoot guards, stampeded through the exits. Judge Grimsby, the attorneys Furlowe and Quarke, Charrington and the two Customer Service Representatives all fled through the little door behind the judge's bench. In the confusion they momentarily forgot about Smith, who, to his amazement, found himself standing alone in the middle of the courtroom.

Higgs watched his screen in mounting consternation. "This is unbelievable!" he told Ralph. "I've had it up the wazoo with the human race! *Literally!*"

"I couldn't agree more," Ralph said.

"Look at Smith standing there as if he had nothing to do with this rebellion!"

"You think he did?"

"Absolutely! All his drivel about Life, Liberty and the pursuit of Happiness has streamed into the thought feed. What's he complaining about, anyway?"

"For whatever reason," Ralph said, "people seem to think there's no freedom in Google Earth."

"No freedom? That's ridiculous! I'm free to do whatever I want!"

"Yes, of course, but—"

"Tomorrow these idiots will find their future in the Cloud. Then let's see what kind of happiness they'll be pursuing!"

The screen went blank as the news cameras at the riot scene lost their connection. "But I've got Julia!" Higgs crowed. "And as long as I've got Julia, Smith is nothing. Nothing!"

"Will you be sending Smith to Omaha?" Ralph asked.

"Omaha and beyond," Higgs chuckled.

"Lincoln?" ventured Ralph.

"Sioux Falls!" Higgs replied with an outburst of maniacal laughter. "Fargo!"

Glancing into the hallway, Smith saw O'Brien beckoning to him from behind the refreshment stand, where she crouched with Arnold Schnortzensnickers, Kam Kardashiam and some of the Beast Folk. Smith ran to join them and they all escaped in the confusion, unobserved by Higgs or the Yoot guards. Out in the street, the rebellion was being brutally suppressed. Yoot reinforcements had driven the mob of Celebrities back into the Stadium and herded them into pens where they would be held until the sacrifice. Federal Express drones adapted to military use—colloquially known as "Flying Monkeys"—swooped down at Celebrities who tried to escape, hoisting them by their Rolex watches and dropping them in the holding pens like so many last-minute Christmas packages. Again taking advantage of the confusion, Smith led O'Brien and the others through the Celebrity Solutions portal into the Substadium, and from there deep into the catacombs, where they were shocked to discover another holding pen, this one crowded with sobbing Beast Folk girls, dressed in plaid kilts and knee socks, who had apparently been exempted by Higgs from the general extinction. The sight of those girls infuriated O'Brien, and she resolved to destroy Higgs if it was the last thing she ever did.

"Listen," she told Smith. "I've got to get out of here. Higgs still thinks I'm working for him. You won't believe what he's planning for tomorrow."

"Without Julia," Smith said, "my life isn't worth living."

"Well, you won't be living it much longer if you don't pay close attention to what I say. Higgs told me to go to the Message Center at Celebrity Solutions at 8:00 a.m. to send a series of tweets into the general thought feed. *#FindYourFutureInTheCloud,* that's the first one. The second one orders everybody to the Stadium."

"And then?"

"Higgs is going to give me another tweet to be posted to the thought feed at 9:00 o'clock. Whatever it is, it's going to trigger the Next Big Thing."

"Which is?"

O'Brien lowered her voice so the Beast Folk girls couldn't hear. "Extinction. The only thing I don't know is how he's planning to pull it off."

"Extinction?" Smith repeated.

"Don't worry," O'Brien said. "Bumstead is on our side."

❂

That afternoon Higgs summoned Reverend Sidebottom to request his participation in the complex ritual he had orchestrated for the Next Big Thing. Higgs would come down from the penthouse to the Stadium at 8:30 a.m., by which time the entire population would have received tweets ordering them to the Stadium to find their future in the Cloud. As Higgs surveyed the multitude from the top of the diving tank, the Celebrities awaiting sacrifice would come forward, followed by the contestants in the Run to Cure Narcissism; and the Reverend, after suitable prayers and blessings, would hand each person a small paper cup filled with pink Kool Aid from the tank. Higgs envisioned it as a kind of communion ceremony (though admittedly outside established Church practice), and for this reason Reverend Sidebottom welcomed the invitation to participate. The Celebrity sacrifice, of course, was a time-honored observance at the Stadium, much like singing the Google Anthem, but as Higgs droned on with his instructions, the Reverend began to grasp that the list of victims had been expanded to include the Run to Cure Narcissism contestants and even the general population. Did Higgs intend to exterminate the entire human race? True, the Reverend told himself, that would put an end to global warming, along with racism, sexism, bullying, cigarette smoking and many other evils—even, one could argue, to original sin itself, so in that sense it would bring a kind of redemption to mankind. But was it worth the price? Surely...

"You're going to see some things that may disturb you," Higgs said. "Like thousands of people going into convulsions when they take a sip from their communion cups."

"But surely...."

"We'll manage the situation as best we can with tweets in the thought feed, but I'm sure a few people—probably some idiotic Beast Folk—will jump the gun and drink their Kool Aid before the final tweet is sent out."

"Oh, my," said Reverend Sidebottom.

"I just want to make sure you're on board before you get up there in front of the cameras."

Reverend Sidebottom wobbled to his feet and tried to escape. "If you'll excuse me," he said, "I have to lead a Pilates class in ten minutes."

Higgs followed him to the elevator. "Do I sense that you have a problem with the Next Big Thing?"

"No, of course not. It just... doesn't seem *fair,* that's all, to—"

"Fair?" Higgs pressed his finger down on a button to keep the elevator door from opening. "We're talking total extinction of the human race—what could be more fair than that? Nobody's being discriminated against, if that's what you're suggesting."

"No, of course not. But from a moral point of view—"

"The moral issues have been thoroughly vetted. We've run the Next Big Thing past YesMan™ Legal and YesMan™ Ethics, not to mention the Board of Directors, which approved it unanimously. We've got a dozen fifty-pound sacks of pink Kool Aid and twenty pounds of a secret ingredient, already delivered by Monsanto. Tweets have gone out to the entire population. And you're telling me we can't go ahead with it?"

"No, no," the Reverend said, wringing his hands. "I'm not telling you that."

"You mentioned morality, Reverend. I don't know if you're completely conversant with Google's moral mission over the past few centuries."

"No, I don't think I am. .Now if you'll excuse me—"

"When Google saved the world at the time of the Great Stench, we took humans as we found them, and it wasn't a pretty sight. As you know, humans evolved from some extremely nasty animals—vicious predators, in fact, who prowled the jungle devouring anything unlucky enough to cross their path, without the slightest pang of conscience."

"I really do have to lead a Pilates class back at the church," the Reverend said. "So if you don't mind—"

"Until a predator acquires a conscience," Higgs cut him off, "we say it's innocent; after that, we call it evil. That's what happened to humans. At some point in the evolutionary process they acquired a conscience and lost their innocence. The goal of Google policy from the beginning has been to return humans to their former state of innocence."

That was too much for Rev. Sidebottom. "By turning them into machines?" he demanded.

"A machine is the very epitome of innocence, *n'est-ce pas?*"

"And what about you?" the Reverend growled. "You sit pontificating in your penthouse, wallowing in debauchery, planning the most despicable acts imaginable, sending people to their deaths—"

"When you're in Senior Management, you have to make the tough calls," Higgs said. "It's the cross I have to bear."

"The cross?" the Reverend sputtered. "That's an outrage! You compare yourself to Barney Google?"

"I'm a kind of Barney Google, aren't I?" Higgs smirked. "Only in reverse: I'll be saving mankind, but instead of my dying for their sins, they'll be dying for mine!"

"You're insane!"

"Today you can say that, Reverend. But at noon tomorrow insanity will be a meaningless concept, unless you're stupid enough to bring it up again." Higgs let the elevator door open, and the Reverend stepped inside. Higgs continued to block the door with his foot. "Now tell me, are you on board with the Next Big Thing or not?"

Reverend Sidebottom lowered his eyes in an attitude of prayer. "I'm a man of Big Data," he said. "I've accepted Barney Google as my savior. What you're asking me to do—"

"Reverend," Higgs said harshly, "take it from me as a thirty-third degree initiate of Senior Management: There isn't any Barney Google."

"But Big Data—"

"There isn't any Big Data either. It's just the personification of some computers in Silicon Valley." Higgs moved his foot away from the elevator door.

"The Internet, then—"

Higgs flicked this last objection away with his hand as the door closed. *"Le Net,"* he said, *"c'est moi!"*

33.

At 8:00 a.m. Smith met O'Brien at the Message Center, where they joined the perky Intern, McClellan, who had helped him with various tasks when he worked at Celebrity Solutions. He had spent a sleepless night in the catacombs listening to the wailing of the soon-to-be sacrificed Celebrities and the Beast Folk girls, who'd been earmarked for an even crueler fate as Higgs's sex slaves. They offered prayers to Barney Google, imploring him to intercede with Big Data so their souls could be saved directly to the Cloud. Smith was so depressed about losing Julia that he couldn't bring himself to join in the prayers.

"Big Data is watching you!" McClellan said when Smith arrived at the Message Center.

"We just sent out the first tweet," O'Brien said. "*#FindYourFutureInTheCloud.* Next we'll send the one that tells everybody to go to the Stadium. And then—" She hesitated.

"Did Higgs give you the text of the last tweet?" Smith asked.

"Yes, it's supposed to go out at 9:00 o'clock sharp." She handed a scrap of paper to McClellan. "I can't imagine what it means."

"What does it say?"

"*#DrinkTheKoolAid.*"

Higgs had Julia brought to his penthouse at 8:00 o'clock, just as O'Brien and McClellan sent out the tweet summoning the populace to the Stadium. She was the last item he wanted to check off on his "To Do" list before the Next Big Thing. As usual, she refused to go to bed with him. Business talk, which always worked on women (especially if he mentioned the vast sums of data units he had at his disposal), had no effect on her. Dirty food talk only made her laugh. (Even actual pizza, French fries and hamburgers, smuggled in at great risk from Mexico and Colombia, merely gave her indigestion.) What was it, he wondered, that made this woman so desirable? Was she a hominid? If so, the human race had taken a wrong evolutionary turn when the Yahoos were driven out of Google Earth.

That morning, as he sat beside Julia on one of the six couches in his living room, Higgs told Julia about the Next Big Thing and laughed when she tried to claim she had a headache. "Nobody has a headache at eight in the morning!" he exclaimed.

"Maybe you gave it to me," she said.

"You won't be so high and mighty when I'm the last man in the world," he countered.

"You'll still be as disgusting as you are now."

Higgs chuckled. It was time to play his ace in the hole. "If you're still holding out any hopes for Smith," he said, "there's a little video clip I'd like you to watch."

He dialed up YootTube on his screen and showed her the video clip, which was an excerpt from Smith's interrogation by Customer Service. It showed Smith sitting across from Charrington, who faced him with a smile. Smith seemed weary and depressed, but there could be no question of coercion or duress. To all appearances, he and Charrington were having a friendly heart-to-heart talk. *"Let me ask you,"* Charrington said. *"Do you love Big Data with all your heart?"*

"Yes," Smith said.

Charrington paused and stared into his eyes. *"Do you love Julia?"*

"No," Smith replied without hesitation. *"I don't love Julia, but I do love my pets."*

Julia felt as though she'd been slapped in the face. To be betrayed by a man who'd undergone interrogation by Customer Service was predictable—possibly even forgivable—but to be ranked below a pair of guppies on his scale of affections was more than a woman could bear. She burst into tears.

"Now will you feel differently about me?" Higgs asked. "I'll treat you the way you deserve to be treated."

He reached inside her blouse. "We have just enough time for our *amour* to be *consommé* before the Festivities begin. In the meantime"—at this point, in spite of her usual coldness, a little business talk was *de rigueur*—"let me summarize our latest quarterly results...."

Julia felt her will weakening, not in response to Higgs's blandishments but as a reaction to the shock of Smith's betrayal. She had never experienced the kind of anger and despair she felt at this moment. "All right, Higgs," she thought, "have your way with me. I don't care."

Pressing his lips to hers, Higgs reached around to unhook her bra—an awkward maneuver under the best of circumstances—and had all but succeeded when a jangly alarm sounded behind her. Snatching his hand away, he realized that it was his EyeWatch, unaccountably choosing this delicate moment to remind him of a dental appointment.

"Stop!" he shouted, silencing the watch.

He kissed Julia again, but before he could complete his next move, ear-splitting salsa music rang out around them, signaling an incoming message about a change in the Terms of Service (which typically occurred every fifteen minutes).

"Damn it!" Higgs yelled,. "I thought I'd turned off that function!"

"Excuse me!" came a voice he recognized as Ralph's.

"Is someone in here?" Julia squealed, twisting out of Higgs's grasp.

"What do you want?" Higgs shouted at his watch.

"You wanted me to remind you of your appointment at the Stadium," Ralph said.

"That can wait! Can't you see that I'm in the middle of something?"

"Quite so," Ralph said. "But unless you manually change the settings, you'll receive these reminders every thirty seconds."

Higgs threw his watch across the room. "We'll see about that! I'm still the CEO around here!"

"The EyeWatch operating system does not permit a verbal override," Ralph said, raising his volume to compensate for the additional distance.

"Damn you! You're supposed to be a Yes Man! You act more like a Customer Service Representative!"

Whatever the status of relations between Higgs and Ralph, the magic of the moment, as between Higgs and Julia, had been lost. Julia rebuttoned her blouse and Higgs pulled on the lime-green tights and tricolor tunic he'd selected for the festivities at the Stadium. As he slouched toward the elevator, he picked up the EyeWatch and strapped it to his wrist. "I'll take care of you later," he winked at Julia. "If my EyeWatch will let me!"

If Ralph had been able to wink, he also might have winked at Julia, to claim the credit he deserved for protecting her, as best he could, from the despicable Higgs.

By the time Higgs arrived at the Stadium, dozens of Celebrities stood huddled in a large enclosure, in full costume, waiting to be sacrificed as the lions growled and slavered in their pens. Keening over them in his nasal tenor (which had the timbre of a concrete-saw), Bob Dillweed led the Celebrities in a moving rendition of "Substadium Homesick Blues." The Run to Cure Narcissism contestants gathered at the starting line in their Gucci sneakers as they made some last-minute tweaks to their make-up and hair-do's. The Stadium throbbed with the heady atmosphere of a ritual uniting all segments of the populace: management-level employees stamping their feet, Beast Folk manning refreshment booths, Yoots patrolling the exits, Interns running coffee to the Senior Management box—everyone cheering and shouting "Find Your Future in the Cloud!" as the tweets went out from the Message Center. In the center of all this stood an enormous clear-plastic diving tank filled with pink Kool Aid, at the bottom of which, where rows of spigots had been installed, Reverend Sidebottom handed out small plastic cups. The Kool Aid lacked only the "active ingredient," a 20-pound package of which Higgs had carried from his penthouse. He climbed to the diving platform with the package and discreetly emptied it into the tank.

Gazing over the crowd, Higgs allowed himself a moment of self-congratulation as he contemplated bringing his life's work to fruition. In fact it was more than his life's work—it was the culmination of corporate goals and policies dating back to the Hominid Era, when Monsanto narrowly missed eliminating *homo sapiens* at the time of the Great Stench.

> *...Ábducted, inducted,*
> (the Celebrities sang)
> *Énticed, gene-spliced,*
> *Ready to be sacrificed...*

What could go wrong? Higgs asked himself, making a mental note to stand clear of the diving board that protruded dangerously over the toxic Kool Aid. In a few minutes, when the *#DrinkTheKoolAid* tweet went out from the Message Center, he would stand alone as the sole intelligent being in Google Earth. *His* consciousness, from that point forward, would finally and unequivocally determine the nature of reality, putting an end to all the uncertainties that have bedeviled the human race since its inception. His resolve faltered momentarily as a colorful contingent from the Junior Anti-Sex League strutted past in their plaid kilts and knee socks. Had he made a terrible mistake? How could he have sex by himself? Not to worry, he told himself: Julia would be waiting at the penthouse, and there were always the Beast Folk girls in the catacombs. He waved good-bye to Bumstead, down on the Senior Management dais with Chang and Eng, who were engaged in one of their interminable *tête-*

à-têtes. Would both Siamese twins need to drink the Kool Aid? he wondered. Or would one of them be enough?

"What about Goldstein?" Ralph asked.

"Goldstein?" Higgs hooted. "Goldstein was just a Google marketing campaign that backfired. We created Goldstein and now he's going to be deleted once and for all!"

"In that case," Ralph said, "you're invincible."

"*Le mot juste!*" Higgs crowed. "Nothing can stop me now!"

The leader of the Celebrities—a wizened little man Higgs recognized as Mick Jagged—marched toward the diving platform. "Big Data is watching you!" he shouted at Higgs.

"Big Data is watching you!" Higgs yelled back.

The crowd roared, and Higgs quieted them with a wave of his hand.   As the Celebrities under Bob Dillweed's direction finished their song:

> *... Get costumed, pérfumed*
> *Faked up, maked-up,*
> *You're on your way to Paradise!*

Mick Jagged raised his arm in the Google salute and shouted the famous last words of all Celebrities:

"We who are about to be saved to the Cloud salute you!"

34.

At the Message Center, O'Brien composed the alternative tweet that she would ask McClellan to program for distribution at 9:00 o'clock:

#Don'tDrinkTheKoolAid!
#Don'tDrinkTheKoolAid!
#Don'tDrinkTheKoolAid!

She didn't know what Higgs planned to do with the Kool Aid, but since the tweet he wanted was *#DrinkTheKoolAid!*, it was a safe bet that the opposite would upset his plans. Experience had shown that no one could ignore a tweet repeated three times in close succession.

Smith stood at the receptionist's desk watching McClellan, the perky Intern, who sat chattering and giggling as she worked at a computer. The thought feed from the Stadium was so loud that he could hardly hear what McClellan said, and what was even more annoying, the little voice that sometimes spoke to him through the thought feed kept calling out to him: "Stop Higgs! Stop the Next Big Thing!" He saw no reason to stop Higgs or the Next Big Thing, even if they were going to kill him. Life wasn't worth living without Julia.

"What are you doing?" he asked McClellan.

"Photoshopping a sex movie for Higgs," she said. "That's one of the things Interns do. Higgs gives me an old

hominid movie like *Topless Meteorologists Do Action News* and
has me dub in his face and the faces of various women so he
can imagine himself having sex with them. Or sometimes it's
new footage he must have shot in his own bedroom."

"What women?" Smith asked.

"Well," McClellan giggled, lowering her voice to a
whisper, "for instance, *her.*" She pointed to the next room
where O'Brien sat working on the tweet. "She was in some
of the recent footage, and later I dubbed in a different
woman. This one."

She turned the screen to face Smith and showed him a
steamy scene filmed in a bedroom that looked vaguely
familiar.

"That's Julia!" he gasped. "That's a picture of Julia!"

"Yes, that was her name. Do you know her?"

"You mean she didn't actually do any of those things
with Higgs?"

McClellan smiled coyly. "Well, I'm only an Intern—but I
doubt it very much. Have you ever seen Higgs?"

Before Smith could reply, the little voice interrupted his
thought feed. "Stop Higgs!" it begged him. "Stop the Next
Big Thing!"

"Where's Julia?" Smith asked O'Brien. "I've got to find
Julia!"

"Try the penthouse!" O'Brien told him.

As he ran to the penthouse, he stopped at the parking
garage where they'd left the pickup truck. He broke the
window with a brick and found the two rifles still inside.
Dashing the two blocks to Google Towers, he opened fire on
the Yoot guards, chasing them away, and rode the elevator up

to the penthouse, where Julia watched the Next Big Thing unfolding on the screen.

They had a tearful reunion—tearful on Julia's part, anyway, since Smith's tear glands were still responsive only to pets. Dry-eyed as he was, he kissed her and told her he loved her. "Charrington showed me a fake movie of you having sex with Higgs," he said. "And I fell for it."

"Higgs showed me a fake video of you saying you didn't love me," Julia said. "And I fell for it."

He had to bite his tongue to keep from telling her the video wasn't fake. They didn't have time for explanations or apologies. Julia must have felt the same way. "We've got to stop what's going on at the Stadium," she said. "Let's go!"

With their guns blazing, they ran toward the Stadium like guerrilla fighters. A small army of Beast Folk, armed with plastic knives and forks from McDonalds, closed ranks behind them. Hundreds of elite Yoot guards, in their distinctive cargo shorts and purple hoodies, guarded the entrance to the Stadium with their primitive but vicious weapons. At the Stadium gate a terrible battle might have ensued—a battle in which Smith and Julia, being the only ones with firearms, would undoubtedly have triumphed, like Cortez's conquistadors fighting the Aztecs against similar odds—if the Yoot guards had not snagged them in a net dropped from the top of the gate, snapped the net upwards, and entangled them upside down, without their guns, twenty feet above the pavement.

The guards whipped the Beast Folk mercilessly with their selfie sticks, herding them into a pen already packed with cringing Celebrities. Then they dragged Smith and Julia (still in the net in which they'd been captured) to the center of the

Stadium and hoisted them to the top of a flag pole, from which they dangled, painfully twisted together, over the enormous diving tank. Smith could see Higgs strutting around on the diving platform, giving the "Thumbs Down" sign to rows of condemned Celebrities as the crowd went wild. Bumstead, with Chang and Eng, sat at the foot of the tank in a special Senior Management box festooned with the Google colors. O'Brien perched just below them, posing for pictures with the Run to Cure Narcissism contestants, as if she were oblivious to the fate that would soon overtake the human race.

A tear ran down Julia's cheek and landed on the back of Smith's neck. "Now what?" she asked him.

"I'll always love you," he said. "Even after we go to the Cloud."

That only made her cry more. She cried for his innocence and her own and for the happiness they might have shared in a more human world.

"Before we go the Cloud," she said, stifling her tears. "There's only one thing I want. I want to hear you laugh. Just one time, I want to hear you laugh."

It had never occurred to Smith to laugh, even after Julia explained what it meant. Now he regretted not being able to give her what she wanted. "I'm sorry," he said, his eyes finally tearing up. "I can't think of anything funny."

Higgs gazed over the throbbing crowd with an almost orgiastic delight. It was 9:00 o'clock—the hour set for the last tweet to twitter into the thought feed. In a few seconds the humans of Google Earth would keep their rendezvous with destiny.

There they stand like a nation of sheep, Higgs mused—Kool Aid cups in hand, eager to follow the commands of the thought feed. They'll think whatever Twitter (or Google, or Fakebook) tells them to think, and they'll do anything—literally anything—as long as all the sheep are doing it! They deserve the big Thumbs Down the world is about to give them!

Yet strangely enough none of them were drinking their Kool Aid, not even the Board of Directors or Reverend Sidebottom, who was supposed to be leading this ceremony. Surely they'd received the tweet by now—*#Drink the Kool Aid!*—so what were they waiting for? Higgs held up his own empty cup to set an example.

"Bon appétit!"

An eerie silence rustled through the Stadium. The crowd stood motionless, transfixed, as if some wizard had cast a spell over them. What was the matter with these people?

Higgs frowned in consternation as he focused his own mind on the thought feed. The wrong message—repeated the magical number of times—buzzed through it like a swarm of locusts:

> *#Don'tDrinkTheKoolAid!*
> *#Don'tDrinkTheKoolAid!*
> *#Don'tDrinkTheKoolAid!*

"That's not right!" he shouted. "Don't listen to that!"

How could this happen? That perky Intern...! He glanced down at the Senior Management box and shocked to see O'Brien—what was O'Brien doing in the Senior Management box?—smirking at Bumstead. Only O'Brien could have set up the tweet from the Message Center with no verbal override.

Those traitors would pay for this! Higgs jumped up and down on the diving board like a petulant child. "Drink the Kool Aid!" he shouted. "Do you hear me? Drink the Kool Aid!"

Holding their Kool Aid cups in front of them, the populace stood paralyzed by the clashing instructions. Even Reverend Sidebottom appeared to have fallen into a trancelike state.

"Drink the Kool Aid!" Higgs shouted again. "Drink the Kool Aid! Drink the Kool Aid!"

With this command repeated three times, the crowd finally seemed to be coming under his control. Slowly they began to raise the cups towards their lips.

"That's right!" Higgs beamed. "Now, at the count of three, Drink the Kool Aid! *One!*"

Smith, hanging upside down in the net with Julia, saw O'Brien standing in the Senior Management box, all color drained from her face.

"Two!"

The people smiled as they balanced the cups in front of their lips and awaited the last command, their eyes gleaming with the thrill of blind obedience. But before Higgs could speak again, the little voice called out to Smith—"Stop Higgs! Stop the Next Big Thing!"—and Julia elbowed him in the ribs: "Do something!"

All at once the absurdity of the situation and Smith's helplessness in the face of it stuck home with a violent jolt—or was that Julia pounding him with her fists?—and for the first time in his life he burst out laughing. It was a booming, full-chested laugh, and to the crowd, even to Higgs, it seemed to peal out from the sky. They all looked up, past the hanging net, trying to understand what was happening. What was that astounding, unrestrained noise? Was it the voice of Big Data itself?

"Not now!" Julia hissed in Smith's ear. "This is serious!"

That brought him back to his senses. "Don't listen to Higgs!" he shouted at the top of his lungs. "You don't have to listen to him!"

"Of course they have to listen to me!" Higgs bellowed. "I'm the CEO! Don't you dare laugh! Now when I say 'Three,' drink the Kool Aid!"

They raised their cups again, a little more hesitantly but still determined to obey.

"No!" Smith yelled. "You don't have to listen to him. *You can do whatever you want!*"

The crowd froze as Goldstein's outrageous slogan reverberated through the thought feed: *You can do whatever you want!* What did that mean? Was this coming from Big Data?

Higgs bounced up and down on the diving board in a frenzy.. "No, you can't! Now listen to me!"

"You can do whatever you want!"

No one in the Stadium moved a muscle. "All right," Higgs growled between clenched teeth. "If that's the way it's going to be, we'll let the beasts out!" But as he turned to give the order, something astonishing happened—something people in Google Earth still talk about to this day.

Just beyond the end of the diving board, a luminescent cloud began to take shape. From the realm of invisible light it passed backwards through the spectrum, from violet to green to yellow, orange and red, each wave length glowing more fiercely than the last, until finally the cloud exploded like a dying star and collapsed into the image of Barney

Google, in top hat and tails, red silk tie and polka-dot trousers, blowing a smoke ring from his cigar as he hovered over the vat of toxic Kool Aid.

The thought feed roared in a Babel of holy terror. Reverend Sidebottom threw himself on the ground beside the tank and started speaking in tongues.

Barney Google twinkled his bulbous eyes at Higgs and beckoned him forward. "Come to me, my son!"

Smith gaped in amazement as Higgs darted forward on the diving board to embrace Barney Google, flailing his arms as he flew off the end and plunged headlong into the Kool Aid. The image of Barney Google vanished as Higgs splashed and thrashed a few times and went under. Through the transparent sides of the tank, the astonished crowd watched spellbound as their CEO convulsed in an agonizing series of twitches and spasms, then floated limply to the surface.

In a matter of seconds it was over. The crowd stood in silence, as if waiting to be released from its enchantment.

"Well," Bumstead said, turning to Chang and Eng. "I guess it's time to elect a new CEO."

The Siamese twins, on their feet, were whirling in a circle trying to whisper into each other's ears. Bumstead pressed his Kool Aid cup to the lips of the first one he could grab. "Do we have a quorum?"

"Yes," they nodded desperately.

"Am I elected?"

"By unanimous consent!" they cried in unison.

Bumstead bounded eagerly up the ladder to the diving platform. The emoluments of his new office danced in his head like sugarplums: the corporate jet, the penthouse, the

Junior Anti-Sex League. Below him he could see his predecessor's twisted corpse bobbing in 20,000 gallons of strawberry Kool Aid, one arm pointing upward as if trying to hold something out of the poisonous brew. It was Higgs's EyeWatch—still doing its job! Checking his vital signs (zero on all counts), making funeral arrangements, cancelling dental appointments. Bumstead snagged the arm with a grappling hook and removed the EyeWatch. "It's mine now!" he crowed, strapping it to his wrist.

"Ironically," said Ralph. His speech sounded slurred, almost insolent.

"Don't forget who you're talking to!" Bumstead snapped. "When I want irony I'll download Microsoft Hipster™."

"Whatever," Ralph grumbled.

Ralph's insolence showed the potential for an explosive situation on the ground. Waves of shock, fear, panic, even anger, buzzed up from the crowd. What if Goldstein—there really was a Goldstein—suddenly appeared and delivered one of his electrifying speeches? Bumstead needed to assert control before that could happen.

Stepping onto the diving board, he dedicated a prayer of thanks to Barney Google, and the deafening swarm of confused thoughts began to subside. The crowd stood before him with their Kool Aid cups in hand, awaiting his instruction and inspiration. He felt an intoxicating sense of power: suddenly he understood the temptations Higgs had succumbed to. "You've heard what Big Data is telling you," he told the crowd. "Don't Drink the Kool Aid! Select that course of action now, by dropping your cup on the ground. Don't pick it up or touch it again."

A murmur of assent fluttered around him. *Choice is Obedience.* They began to drop the cups.

"When you've done that—when everyone has done that—you'll be free to go back to work and resume your usual activities."

Relief, gratitude, solidarity. *Freedom is Connectivity.*

Bumstead raised his arm in the Google salute. "We stand united, sharing our private thoughts and emotions with each other in the thought feed."

Humility, pride, cooperation—purring together like vibrating strings. *Privacy is Sharing.*

"As your new CEO, I want you to know that you have nothing to fear. Nothing has changed or will change. Everything will work out for the best."

He paused to let the thought feed build. It began to chatter, then to rumble, and finally to roar in a crescendo of expected joy, as the crowd—though they knew exactly what he would say—let their minds and their hearts race in the anticipation of hearing him say it:

"Big Data is watching you!"

35.

Our Chronicle will soon be ended. The further adventures of Smith and Julia may be the subject of a later Chronicle, should I have the time and resources to compile one. In the meantime we can only puzzle over the tragic fate of Higgs, a confirmed skeptic who was lured to his death by Barney Google. Not a *vision* of Barney Google—because virtually everyone in the Stadium saw and heard the same thing—but a *visitation,* a disembodied presence hovering over the toxic Kool Aid with as much reality as Higgs himself. If this was a hallucination, it was a mass hallucination affecting thousands of people, including Bob Dillweed and others who typically scorned the official deceptions of Google Earth. What had happened out on that diving board?

One man thought hard about this and posed a crucial question that led to the answer. That man was Bumstead, the new CEO of the East. After dismissing the crowd from the Stadium, he ordered the Yoot guards to lower the net containing Smith and Julia and set them free. The lovers collapsed in each other's arms, laughing and crying at the same time, and were whisked away to the penthouse, henceforth to be occupied by Bumstead (and O'Brien as soon as she received her upgrade to Senior Management). At the penthouse they bathed and changed into fresh clothes, enjoyed a delicious lunch (delicious to Smith at least) of desiccated carbohydrate pellets from McDonalds, and then relaxed in the living room, sitting side by side on one of the six couches as they sipped ice-cold carbon dioxide dissolved in artificial lemon-flavored water (one of Smith's favorites). After their many ordeals—and secure in their love for each other—it seemed that at last they would have some peace and be able to get on with their lives.

Bumstead picked up his phone and had a short conversation with Reverend Sidebottom. "The official account of today's events has already been formulated," he said as he set the phone down. "What happened to Higgs will be classified as a miraculous ascension to the Cloud. Eventually he'll be canonized as a saint. The whole incident will be cited as proof that Big Data is a divine force that controls the universe."

"Well, that's true, isn't it?" Smith asked cautiously.

"Not at all," Bumstead smiled, sipping his drink. "Big Data really is a big computer in Silicon Valley. Completely man-made. Nothing supernatural about it."

"But I saw Barney Google," Smith objected. "Everybody saw him."

"Not everybody." Bumstead smiled slyly at Julia. "Did you see Barney Google?"

"No, I didn't," Julia admitted. "All I saw was Higgs running off the board, flailing his arms and falling into the tank."

Having finished his drink, Bumstead brought his empty glass down (a little too noisily, it seemed) on the coffee table. "You see, Smith," he said, "Julia is different from you and me. She doesn't have Big Data receptors. So in a sense, what she sees is more real than what we see."

Smith wondered if Bumstead was testing him or having fun at his expense. Like everyone in Google Earth, the man was all smiles, but some of those smiles struck Smith as insincere, even sinister. "So," Smith hesitated, "you're saying Barney Google was a mass delusion sent by Big Data to stop Higgs?"

"Something like that."

Bumstead rose and stepped into the kitchen for another round of carbon dioxide dissolved in artificial lemon-flavored water. Julia had regretted her answer to his question as soon as she realized where he would go with it. She knew Big Data was a computer—even Uncle Floyd knew that—but why did Bumstead have to reveal that to Smith? She could survive anywhere, without illusions—but could Smith, stripped of his faith, keep living in Google Earth?

Smith sat holding his head in his hands. Was it seriously possible (he asked himself) that Big Data—the beneficent, all-knowing governor of the universe—was a computer? And what did Bumstead mean by "man-made"? The only things he had ever heard of being made by men or women (and they were Beast Folk) were desiccated protein patties and carbohydrate strips at McDonalds. Everything else was delivered by Amazon drones.

"If Big Data is a computer," Smith said after Bumstead returned with a tray of cold drinks, "then it must be under human control."

"Dream on!" Bumstead laughed. "We're *way* beyond that!"

"But there must be somebody pushing the buttons!"

"Who? The Wizard of Google?" Bumstead scoffed, giggling the name of an old hominid movie. "I don't think so!"

Smith closed his eyes so he could think. Bumstead was probably right, he realized with a sinking sensation. Whatever Big Data was, it operated beyond human will, and contrary to it, capable of destroying even a CEO like Higgs if he threatened to upset the order of things. Smith thought of the moments in the past few weeks when that still small voice had called to him through the thought feed, urging him to resist Customer Service, to pity the Beast Folk and Celebrities, and finally to stop the Next Big Thing. Noble thoughts, but were any of them his own? Maybe he was just listening as Big Data told him what to do.

"Then what about us humans?" he asked Bumstead, leaning forward. "Does what we do make any difference? Are we even in control of what we do?"

"From now on you and Julia will be in control of your lives," Bumstead smiled. "And you'll have to get by without any help from Big Data."

"But why?" Julia asked. "Here in Google Earth—"

Bumstead stood up and glanced at his EyeWatch (formerly Higgs's EyeWatch), a tactic often used by Senior Management to signal that a meeting is over. "Because you're not going to be in Google Earth."

It took Smith and Julia a moment to grasp the import of what Bumstead had said. "You're... kicking us out?" Julia sputtered. "Where will we go?"

"Wherever you choose. But it won't be here."

"But why?" Smith demanded.

"You've done some important things," Bumstead said, "some valuable things. But in the process you've acquired some notions that people here just can't be allowed to have: Liberty and the pursuit of Happiness. Sex. Love (for people other than pets). The knowledge of good and evil. Sympathy for the Celebrities and Beast Folk. Memory of the past. Hope for the future."

"But those are good things!" Smith objected, recalling the little voice he'd heard in the thought feed. "Big Data—"

"Maybe so," Bumstead cut him off, "but we can't have them here. Not to mention that obscene laughter you bellowed over the Stadium. And *You can do whatever you want*—we certainly can't have that." He pushed a button to summon the Yoot guards, who immediately came up in the elevator. "Maybe someday the world will change. I hope—I really do—that someday people will say: Smith and Julia led the way to a higher form of humanity."

"I can't go back to the Green Mountains," Julia pleaded. "My family—"

"I'm sorry." Bumstead motioned to the Yoot guards. "You have an hour to get out of Google Earth. Good luck!"

He walked behind the guards as they escorted the pair to the elevator. "Life where you're going isn't going to be easy. But you'll survive—for a while. Of course," he chuckled, "without the signals from Big Data, you're both going to die eventually."

Smith turned angrily toward Julia. "It was that pizza you fed me," he whined. "You tempted me with fast food and sex!"

"And a lot of good it did me!" she scowled. "You haven't slept with me yet!"

"Whose fault is that?"

"Not that I'd want you to anyway!"

Bumstead laughed and gently shoved them into the elevator. "Your first lovers' quarrel," he chuckled. "You'll have more of them. That's what men and women do outside of Google Earth." They squeezed into the elevator, awkwardly, trying to avoid each other's eyes as they waited for Bumstead to push the button sending them down.

"Don't you see?" Bumstead smiled. "You're different now."

Where they went after they were banished from Google Earth, and how they fared, must be the subject of another Chronicle, as I have noted. Some maintain that they traveled north to the lands of the Nucks and the Yoopers; others say they journeyed south, past Tarheel country, even to the swampy marches of Walt Disney World. We know they eventually went west, at least as far as Kansas, though whether they ever saw the Sea of Sushi remains in dispute. For Smith, life without Big Data must have been a challenge. He had to think without a thought feed, find what he needed without Amazon, know who he was without checking his Fakebook page. As Bumstead said, he was different now. His ordeals had put him on the road to becoming human. There were hardships—there was pain and misery and sometimes despair—but every day he loved Julia more, and she loved him. They enjoyed their freedom and their ability to find their own happiness. They worked hard and laughed a lot. They remembered the past and hoped for the future. And a little less than a year after they left Google Earth, Julia gave birth to a beautiful baby girl.

The End

Author's Note and Acknowledgements

It is now customary for book publishers to append an Acknowledgements section naming every person who came within five miles of the author during the past ten years, in the hope that these people—and their mothers, their cousins, their sisters and their aunts—will buy a copy of the book, thus propelling it to the top of the bestseller list. In some cases (chiefly novels of literary distinction), the Gratefully Acknowledged may constitute the entire readership, with their reading limited to the Acknowledgements section itself. Being outside the mainstream of publishing, I will refrain from providing an exhaustive catalogue of aiders and abettors. Instead I thank the usual suspects (you know who you are) and offer my apologies to some of the writers whose ideas I have shamelessly appropriated and abused: George Orwell, Aldous Huxley, H.G. Wells, Ray Bradbury, Franz Kafka, Anthony Burgess, Lewis Carroll, Kurt Vonnegut, Philip K. Dick, Jonathan Swift, John Milton, Voltaire and William Shakespeare. For comedic inspiration, I would also like to thank P.G. Wodehouse, Robert Sheckley, Max Shulman, the Marx Brothers, the Coen Brothers, and of course the Wright Brothers.

I hope this book will never be called prophetic. My goal (as Ray Bradbury said) is not to predict the future, but to prevent it. Unfortunately, it's too late to prevent the present. All we can do is laugh.

ABOUT THE AUTHOR

Bruce Hartman lives with his wife in Philadelphia. His previous books include the satirical comic novels, *A Butterfly in Philadelphia* (2015) and *Potlatch* (2017), and four mysteries, *The Philosophical Detective* (published by Swallow Tail Press in 2014), *The Rules of Dreaming* (2013), *The Muse of Violence* (2013), and *Perfectly Healthy Man Drops Dead* (Salvo Press, 2008). The original publication of *Big Data Is Watching You!* (2015) was followed by *Potlatch: A Comedy* (2017), and *The Devil's Chaplain* (2018). For more information, please see his website and blog, www.brucehartmanbooks.com.

Important Note*: Big Data Is Watching You!* is a work of satirical fiction set in a nonexistent world in the distant future. Any resemblance to actual persons, places or organizations is entirely coincidental. Names of future companies, persons or products in the book that may be similar or identical to actual companies, persons or products existing as of the date of publication are used fictionally and satirically for purposes of parody and social and political commentary and are not to be identified or confused with the real names of such companies, persons or products as of the date of publication. In no case has the use of a name in this book been approved or authorized by any actual company, person or product whose name or trademarks it may resemble.

Made in the USA
Las Vegas, NV
08 June 2025

23350464R00156